LANA LYNNE

A COMPASS OF STARS IN YOUR EYES

A novel
By

Lana Lynne

ISBN-13: 978-1-0882-6187-3

DEDICATION

My family
&
In Memory of my wonderful in-laws,
Sue and Dick

ACKNOWLEDGMENTS

A Compass of Stars in Your Eyes is a work of historical fiction. All characters are fictional except for historical figures discussed. Any mention or interactions with them are fictional. Please consult the "Author's Notes and Resources for Research and Further Reading" section at the end of this novel. There are no quotes from any of these. I find weaving a background of historical events into fictional lives and situations enriches the story. Any errors or adjustments made in order to develop this work of fiction are my own.

I owe a debt of gratitude to my family, friends, fellow writers, and readers. It began with my first novel in 2009. There are too many to list. However, I must express my appreciation for a few who have kept my pen flowing for this novel.

So many people helped in the research process. I am grateful to those who gave expeditious responses and assistance. Leigh Jeremias, Digital Collections Coordinator, Colorado State Library; the staff, and the librarians at the Longview Public Library in Longview, Texas; Stephanie at the Robert W. Richardson Railroad Library and the staff at the Colorado Railroad Museum; and Gladewater Books in Gladewater, Texas.

I extend my heartfelt gratitude to the members of my critique group from the East Texas Christian Writers' Group: Barbara Arent, Linda Burklin, Vickie Phelps, and Amber Tinsley. Thank you for your candid suggestions and corrections.

I also wish to thank Debra L. Butterfield for her Developmental Edit and suggestions.

A special and infinite appreciation for my supportive husband and family. Rick Higginbotham is honest when the story is not working and encourages me until it does. Our daughter, son-in-law, and granddaughter provide ongoing inspiration.

Stories of heart, heritage, and home characterize my novels. This theme flows from the faith and steadfast love of my parents and in-laws. I am grateful for their legacy and cherish still having my father. My gratitude is endless.

Thank you, Lord. ~ Lana

Chapter One

Whispers and giggles from the trees above turned Jack's gaze upward toward the branches shading his head. A grin found its way onto his face. He would have known his sister-in-law anywhere. She sat on a lower limb with an arm around a young boy who had to be his nephew. After eleven years away from home, he found himself uncertain of many things. A steady barrage of acorns made him dodge and search higher in the tree. An older, dark-haired boy continued his acorn attack from another limb until Jack removed his hat. The younger boy giggled, leaning on his mother. The oldest looked about nine. Jack shook his head.

"He sure looks like Pa," the younger boy said.

Their mother laughed, starting her descent with her youngest. Bits of loosened tree bark hit her face, and she turned her head to the side until her son's feet shared the lower branch with her.

"He *should.* Boys, this is your Uncle Jack," she said.

Their mouths gaped as the two exchanged looks of disbelief. The eldest scrambled ahead of his mother who helped her youngest to safety.

Jack reached up to assist his oldest brother's wife, noting the changes. Light creases accented her dove-colored eyes and her wrinkled dress clung to a more mature figure, but the rest remained unchanged. A sprinkle of freckles remained on her nose and the escaping amber hair strands, always close to disarray during their childhoods, remained the same.

"Still climbing trees, I see. Florey, you sure are a handsome woman. Marcus chose well," he said.

Florence's eyes sparkled as she punched him in the arm.

"Ow!" Jack flinched, looking at his nephews. "She's not eighteen anymore, but some things don't change."

"That's for not stopping by after you visited with our friends in Washington three years ago. You *promised*. It's now late September of 1877, Jack. There's been so much . . . so much," Florence said. Then she hugged him. "*This* is for how happy I am to see you." She stepped back, wiping away a tear.

Jack frowned at the change. His nephews flanked their mother, the youngest buried his face in her skirt and the eldest stared up at Florence with concern on his young face.

"I tried to arrange things, but the railroad had other plans for me during the first year after graduation," Jack said.

Florence's eyes held a message. A sense of foreboding filled him.

"What is it, Florey?"

She shook her head.

Jack gazed down into the now solemn eyes of the boys. He squatted and extended his hand. "I'm your Uncle Jack, your pa's youngest brother."

"I'm Alan Lee Johnson, and this is my brother Elias Richard Johnson. He's five. We're your nephews," the older one said, shaking Jack's hand.

He cleared his throat, the smile he hoped to share with their mother faded as tears coursed down her face. His heart pounded when he turned back to his nephews. "Nice to meet you, boys."

A beautiful older woman with gold-tipped, graying hair pinned in a plaited cornet encircling the top of her head appeared on the porch.

Florence put one hand on each of her sons' shoulders. "Boys, go with your grandma and wash up for lunch. Your pa and the others will get back from town soon."

The older woman came down the stairs. She placed an arm around each of her grandsons and nodded at him. "It's good to see you, Jack. Have you stopped by your family's farm?"

Jack dropped his head and kicked at the dirt. Shoot, he felt like a reprimanded boy again. He guessed some things never changed.

"No, Mrs. Cushman. I stopped by your son's house first, and Jenny said Richard came to help Marc and Mr. Cushman. So I came here, figuring to see him, as well as my oldest brother. I'm not sure if Will and Alice will welcome me at home."

Ella Cushman's lips compressed. The disapproval of this woman, who should have been his mother-in-law, still rankled him. He'd worked for years to be the favored brother. For all the good it'd done him.

"You'd better forget about all the petty competition between you and your brother Will. My youngest daughter chose him. You left home back then. But *now,* your ma needs you."

"Ma, I haven't told him," Florence said.

A flicker of apprehension churned inside of him. "Told me what?"

"Boys, let's go inside." Ella ushered her grandsons up the porch steps. The sound of wagon wheels drew her gaze toward the road before she shut the front door.

The buckboard stopped. Jack waved at the three men with the load of lumber. His eldest brother jumped down and removed his gloves. Florence waited with Jack for her husband to join them.

Marc grinned at him and some of Jack's apprehension ebbed away. This is why he came home—family.

"*Will* can at least *try* to deny relation to me. But you, little brother … it's like looking in a mirror at my younger self," Marc said.

They shook hands.

"Isn't it? He just dresses fancier," Florence said. She bit her lip. "Marc, he hasn't gone home yet." Her gray eyes turned back toward Jack. "Jack, I wish you'd arrived a few days sooner."

Jack expelled his breath, walked a few feet away and set his bag on the steps. He turned back with his arms crossed. "Florence, you're never so guarded in your words. What's happened?"

Marc kissed his wife on the top of her head. "Florey, go on inside and get the letter for me. My brother and I need to take a walk."

Florence patted Jack's shoulder. She returned a few moments later and handed an envelope to Marc. He met Marc's eyes before they turned for the road. Richard and Mr. Cushman waved as he followed Marc past the wagon to the wheel-rutted thoroughfare.

Trepidation silenced him. He matched his brother's steady stride—afraid of where he led, yet somehow, he knew.

The mound of fresh dirt under one of the old trees in the Rockport Cemetery brought confirmation. He twisted the brim of his hat as tears fell. His eyes found the place cleared for the stone. A vise of emotion choked him. He sniffed and swallowed hard, too overcome to face his brother.

"*Pa*? Where's the stone? *When*? What happened?"

"It's being made. Pneumonia got him last week," Marc said in a voice tinged with fresh grief. "Ever since his slow recovery after his fall, the one bringing Florey and me home from Texas, he stayed susceptible to illness. I'm glad I came, or we might not have had him this long. My children got to know him. I didn't know how to locate you. Will telegraphed the last railroad office mentioned in your letter last month."

Shock, grief, and grim acceptance collided.

"I chose to take the chance of never seeing him again," Jack said.

"Yes, you did. I did too, once."

Jack spun around. He searched his brother's face but found no condemnation there, just empathy.

"Uh huh, but they're two different things, Marc. You went to war. After that, you stayed to help a friend."

Marc slumped against the tree with his head back

and his eyes closed. After a moment, he straightened and his eyes met Jack's.

"Yes and no. War, prison, and life taught me the inevitability of death. Only God knows the timing. We must contend with the consequences of our choices. Some right, some wrong, and a few not fitting either. The last one fits your choice. You left home knowing Will and Alice remained here for Ma and Pa. If they left, then you might have . . . there again, I'm the oldest. It fell to me to come home. Will and I have wives and children." He nodded. "Yes, Will and Alice have one here and one on the way. Ma hasn't written to you about everything. So, you see, you're free to find your life away from here. Pa was glad of it."

"Are you sure?"

"Yes. He talked about you with pride—a college graduate in our family. His pride in your intellect made him tolerate Uncle Samuel paying for your school. Because he knew you might be the first. He left a letter for you. Besides, your letters home made his eyes sparkle with adventure. I think we got our wandering feet from him, but he chose to put down roots instead. Now, so have I, but it doesn't mean you have to." Marc pushed off the tree. "Take a spell here. Then head home to see Ma. *She* does need you for the time you're here. I've got work to do."

Jack threw his hat at the tree by his father's grave. Marc turned.

"Do you know why I went by Richard's first?"

Marc returned to the tree, crossed his arms, and leaned his back against it again. He removed his hat and wiped a finger across his dark mustache. A sardonic expression appeared on his face. "To look for

Richard?"

Jack gave a small smile, enjoying the brotherly teasing laced in Marc's question. He lifted his eyebrow.

"Of course. No, beyond the obvious? And, I didn't tell Jenny. I wanted to ask him if I could stay with them."

"Why?"

"Well . . . first, because I can't stay with Alice and Will, but I mean—"

Jack sank down next to the tree as weariness overtook him. He directed his next words toward his father's grave. "I'm coming home, Pa."

His brother slid down beside him. Neither spoke. A rare breeze rustled the early autumn leaves in the tree above them. A few twirled down like the unheeded tears on Jack's face.

"Do you mean *now*, Jack? Is it because of the railroad strike in July? I thought it ended."

Numbness and dazed thoughts delayed Jack's reply. He wiped away the tears on his twenty-six-year-old face, ashamed of the display. "No, the strike is over. The option to do other survey work benefitted me then. No, not this trip, I plan to return home this spring. After a lengthy correspondence with Mr. Reynolds, it appears the southern railroad connections will have a place for me here or in Hot Springs by then. I came to tell Pa and Ma. My current commitments return me to Colorado after this visit. I have to leave in three days."

Marc's green eyes mirrored his own in color and emotion. Jack needed to pace a bit. He sighed and stood. At least his *eldest* brother wanted him home.

"I'm right glad to hear it. Ma will be too. I want you certain about this. Will and I have things handled,"

Marc said.

"Well, I've got plenty of adventures left in me." Jack put his hands in his pockets and started a rapid back and forth volley path in the dirt, like a target in a shooting contest. If his reasons for not coming home before their father's death didn't hold up with his brother, then they'd be unfounded excuses in his mother's and Will's eyes. "The thing is, after visiting with our old friends and meeting new ones in Washington in '74, it got me thinking, especially after meeting Eddie and Hallie. I missed my family, but I'd just graduated and hired on as a railroad surveyor. It didn't work out for me to stop by for a visit because the railroads suffered the residual impact of issues from the panic of '73. My situation with them came after much inquiry, so I couldn't quit after starting—many couldn't even find jobs. I wanted to honor Uncle Samuel's belief in me and to repay him for my schooling."

"Would you get still and look at me, Jack? You're wearing on me," Marcus said. Once Jack walked back and sat next to him, Marcus resumed. "Did you know we finally met Eddie and Hallie this past summer? They made a detour on their way back from picking up his nephew in Texas. Eddie's nephew, Jared, is a fine boy."

An unexpected gust of wind tousled their dark hair—much like the hand of their father in childhood. The kindred moment gripped them, too tender for words. Rustling leaves and memories subsided. Jack swallowed the lump in his throat.

"Yes, Jared is. He still has to travel between his family in Texas and Washington D.C. each year. After *all* he's gone through; he deserves a little happiness. I'd hoped Eddie would join me with the railroad, but he chose better by marrying Hallie."

"She's prettier."

They laughed.

"I agree." Jack glanced back at their father's grave. "As for me—I didn't choose too well."

"Stop it, little brother. The letter in my pocket is to you from Pa. Once I give it to you, take your time reading it. Go see Ma. Get rid of the guilt Will tries to throw on you. Don't blame Alice for choosing Will over you. See, she too made unchangeable choices. Go forward. Florence taught me that, with God's help. It's how I made peace. Timing is a funny thing. We don't regret our time in Texas, and although we miss our friends there, coming back to Arkansas brought peace. If you still feel it's time to come home this spring, we'd love to have you. But, if it's guilt bringing you, don't do it. Pray about it." Marc slapped Jack's knee, nodded as he caught his eye, and unfolded his still lithe form. He removed the envelope from his pocket and held it down to him. "Let Pa tell you how he felt and don't listen to me or anyone else but God and Pa for the truth of it. Goodness knows you're the best-educated family member. I'll tell Richard to expect you tonight. It'll give Will and Alice a bit to adjust to your arrival."

Jack watched his brother head for the old road.

"Thanks, Marc."

The leaves rustled, a lone bird called, and the familiar smell of the rich soil surrounded him—Home. He wiped his nose with the back of his hand and slid the pages bearing his father's rough scrawl from the envelope. The voice, still burned into his memory, read them in his mind, and his heart heard every word.

An hour later, he stood, picked up his bag, and headed to Richard Cushman's home.

Chapter Two

Mina Kolek bit the edge of her fingernail before she stepped down onto the railway platform. A furtive glance backward assured her the man—the charade of a well-dressed gentleman—remained close behind. He boarded at the same time as she did in Denver. She recognized him as one of the regular saloon gamblers in town. How she wished for her uncle at this moment. He'd insisted she travel without him when he fell ill a few days before her departure from Denver. They had teased about this trip since her fifteenth year. She even wrote to him about it while attending college in Illinois. Her cousins there found it a fanciful and silly notion, so she did not mention it again after her first year with them. The fact that her uncle found it worthy sufficed. After all, he'd raised her following her parent's deaths during her fifth year. She trusted his opinion the most. Although, she must admit, if one of her friends proposed such a trip, she too might have laughed.

Traveling across a few states to visit a town because of a chance encounter years ago might give many pause. Her uncle met the young man from Rockport, Arkansas after an explosion trapped the men together in the spring of 1871. What made her uncle advise the young man to leave the railroad and go home? Furthermore, what made Mina so fascinated as to wonder about him all these years? It seemed the youth did not plan to heed her uncle's words from the conversation related. Her uncle said the look in young Jack Johnson's eyes and the tone of his voice when he spoke of home stayed with him. Jack Johnson. Why did she care what happened to him? Why couldn't she plan a future until she knew?

Right now, she cared more about her own safety. Thank goodness her cousin Daniel had coordinated his travel plans to meet her today. She knew the man behind her. He had floated in and out of town since her return from college. Mr. Mathias made her scurry back to her job at the mercantile anytime she met him on the street. She only gave a polite smile to his greetings. College taught her many things, but she learned about the dark nature of man early. Her uncle taught her caution as they passed through mining camps during her childhood. Certain men sent off sparks of fear just by looking at a girl. Mr. Mathias merited rank among them. Her uncle told her to avoid the man. She managed it until boarding the train. It made her rethink the wisdom of traveling alone.

Her eyes scanned the depot platform. Independence turns to folly in an instant. The irritation she had felt when she read her cousin's telegram six weeks ago, changed to gratitude at the sight of him. His refined suit set him apart from many around him. She sighed. Don't look back, she told herself. She hurried forward.

"Daniel." She reached for his outstretched hands. "When did you arrive?"

He took her hands and smiled. "Two days ago. The trip from Illinois found no mishaps. And yours? My sister telegrammed me about Uncle Silas."

Before she could answer, she felt the hair on her neck raise and chills creep up her arms as a deep voice interrupted them.

"Please excuse me, Miss Kolek. I don't believe we've breached formal acquaintance." He bowed. "George Mathias of San Francisco, and Denver, of late. Your dear uncle expressed concern about your travel when I visited the mercantile last week, I promised to keep an eye on you as my business caused my plans to intersect your own. I do hope my presence has not unsettled you."

The explanation did not ring true, but she decided on a gracious response. "How kind of you, Mr. Mathias. My uncle failed to mention your plans to me." She forced a smile as she turned.

The ice blue eyes reflected polished charm to accompany a devilish smile. "Not at all. Now you've found your beau, Mr.—"

"I'm—" Her cousin stopped at the warning glance she gave him. "I'm Daniel Cummings. Let me express my gratitude for your care of Miss Kolek on behalf of her uncle and myself. Please rest assured; she is now safely delivered."

Her cousin's brown eyes revealed nothing as he took her arm. "I'll see to her trunk now. Good day to you, sir."

Neither spoke or glanced back at the man in the silk suit. She waited until Daniel put her in the buggy to glance back at the gambler.

"Uncle Silas did not ask him to watch after you or he would have known about me. I don't like it," Daniel said.

"I'm glad your mother is Uncle Silas's sister."

A puzzled expression settled on his face. "Likewise, but—"

"As she's married, you have a different last name than I do."

"It did work out well." He smiled. "I'm also glad you didn't get the brown eyes I inherited from the Koleks. Otherwise, we could not deny our relation."

"We do resemble otherwise." She bit her lip. "I hope he didn't notice the similarities."

"Who is he?"

"One of the gamblers who frequents Denver."

Daniel flicked the reins. Mina held on and relaxed in her seat. Her eyes took in the lush trees and relished the smell of rich soil in the humid air in this place she'd so longed to reach. Her cousin grunted, and she pulled her gaze away from the scenery.

"I don't like him," Daniel said. He glanced at her and his scowl disappeared. "Anyway, here are my plans. I've allowed us about a week to explore this Rockport and Malvern area fascinating you. If Jack Johnson *is* here, I'm sure he is well settled and married. We will introduce ourselves, send him Uncle Silas's regards, and board the train back to Denver."

"But you don't need to arrive there until next month. We have plenty of time," she said.

She viewed the town with interest. Much smaller than Denver, but it had stores and the signs on the other establishments seemed indicative of most towns.

Daniel pulled up in front of the hotel. Once the horses came to a standstill, he turned to her, his brow furrowed. "I thought our college days taught you reasoning, Cousin. Things are never what we imagine. This will not take long. I don't see why you persisted since Uncle Silas could not travel, but I allow you this one fanciful notion as you've talked about it since I first met you. Life brought us into each other's lives late, but I'm grateful. Look how it's changed things for me. I can now set up my medical practice in Denver and have family close."

Mina glanced at the bustling town. *Why did she come to Malvern, Arkansas?* She nibbled at a rough fingernail.

Daniel reached over and covered her hand. "I'm sorry, Mina. The risks you took traveling here alone unsettles me. We will take all the time you need."

She smiled, excitement flickering in her heart. This trip could decide her future.

"Thank you, Daniel.

Chapter Three

Jack delighted in the expectant faces surrounding the dinner table. His mother sat beside Richard's wife, Jenny Cushman, who sat across from her two children—nine-year-old David and five-year-old Leah. Richard sat next to his brother-in-law John.

"Why didn't you move home when Mr. Reynolds opened the railroad connection to Hot Springs in '75?" Richard asked.

"Well, I thought about it, but so much happened after my brief visit in Washington. The railroads faced many challenges in '74. Some, before I came, like the plague of grasshoppers in Nebraska, and others afterward. My friend Hiram said he'd never seen anything like those insects swarming so bad as to stop a train. I've learned a lot. The country has continued to change with states finally re-entering the Union after the initial delays and even slower return of our local governments. I heard our state got a new constitution in '74."

"We did. I hate politics," Richard said.

"Everything is expanding west. It's exciting and it"—Jack's eyes met Richard's—"comes at a great price. I've learned the nature of men ruled by greed. Life means little to them. I need to come home again."

His mother nodded at Jenny. "Let's get the children to bed. I think the men have more to say than is possible in our company." She stood and moved behind Jack, placing a hand on his shoulder. "Besides, I need to head home soon."

Jack covered the maternal hand with his. "Thanks, Ma. I'll take you home."

She squeezed his hand. "You visit; I want to read a bit with David and Leah before we go."

The children left the room with her as Jenny cleared the table.

John Wilkins, one of his oldest brother's dearest friends, propped both elbows on the table once Jenny removed the empty plate in front of him.

Jack still remembered the long ago June day when Marcus, Richard, and the Wilkins brothers marched away to war. He still missed John's younger brother; so many who left on that well celebrated day did not return home.

"I'm glad I stopped by in time for your delicious pie, Jenny. Thank you."

"Thank you, John. I know Dawn makes splendid pies, too," Jenny said.

Jack grinned. He thought about Florence and Richard's eldest sister. Their families shared so much. "How's your lovely wife, John?"

"Still the greatest gift the Lord's ever given me. She and my children make me a blessed man."

"I won't argue," Jack said.

"At least you're happy for two of my sisters," Richard said.

Jack refused to discuss Richard's third sister with him. Instead, he studied John and Richard from across the table. They grew up with Marc and fought side-by-side during the Civil War.

"John, I visited Fort Delaware."

A despondent darkness flickered for a moment in the other man's eyes.

"That's not a place to visit."

"I wanted to. What I found helped me understand what you, Marc, and Boyd Richards went through as prisoners there during the war."

The brown eyes and kind face of the strapping man hardened. "No—only the other prisoners know. Jack, I grew up thinking of things as either right or wrong. There is an area between the black and white. Many call it gray. I used to disregard it. The war taught me its reality."

Jack didn't blink. "Do you mean things like Boyd getting you and Marc out early due to his uncle's connections?"

"Jack, don't tread there," Richard said.

"You know about it, Richard?"

The red-haired man nodded before he took a sip of coffee. "I didn't until after they came home. Marc told me the night we walked home together after our fight at my pa's. He wanted me to understand everything before he married Florey and left for Texas."

John's eyes bore into him. "Marc and I remained

too sick to make the decision. The so-called transfer they presented to Boyd gave him a way to save us. He knew we lay dying in the infirmary, so he agreed and signed the oath-pledge to the Union for us all. Men either make decisions out of selfishness and meanness or selflessness and love. Those make the difference in those hard to distinguish places."

Jack had never heard John say so much at one time. He nodded.

"You're right, John. The big business men I've worked with are often the selfish and mean variety. I don't want to become like them."

Richard chuckled. "Jack, it's sprinkled around from the lowest to highest. It's here too."

"I know, but at least there are men I can trust close by," Jack said.

"About time you realized it." John smiled and leaned back in his chair. "Now, as to the reason for my visit here tonight—"

Jack frowned. "Didn't Marc send you?"

"Well, in a way. You see, I went to tell Marc what my lovely wife heard in town. He told me you came home and to tell you in person. Anyway, there's a man who's been asking questions about you the last few days in both Rockport and Malvern. A lady who got off the train today joined him. Mrs. Fletcher from the hotel saw Dawn at the mercantile this afternoon and told her about it."

Jack rubbed a hand across the back of his neck and shook his head.

"I don't know why anyone would be looking for me. Maybe it's one of my old college friends and his wife."

"Well, Mrs. Fletcher said the man's name is Daniel Cummings," John said.

Too much travel and grief to think right now, Jack decided. He yawned and rubbed his eyes. "No, no, I don't remember anyone with that name. Maybe he works with the railroad in this area."

John shrugged. "It doesn't seem likely. No one seems to know him in town, and they don't like his questions about you and your family. Anyway, everyone has kept their mouths shut. Mrs. Fletcher thought Marc might want to talk to them. But since you're here—"

"I'll take care of it tomorrow. Mr. Cummings will not bother anyone else. Thank you."

John nodded and stood. "Well, I best get home. Why don't I take your ma by her place?"

"I'm beholden to you, John."

An hour later, Jack walked down to the edge of the Ouachita River, which flowed within sight of Richard's home.

The stars gleamed in the darkened sky. He found a seat on one of the large rocks at the edge. The breeze still held warmth with a bare hint of coolness from the water. Arkansas summers scorched and only gave a grudging passage to autumn.

"The current's a little strong for a swim right now."

He turned at Richard's voice and stood. "Recent rain storms?"

"Some." Richard propped against one of the boulders. "If Will refuses to forgive you, what happens?"

Jack skipped a rock across a still place in the swirling water surface. "I'm not sure. It's odd, because he ended up with your sister Alice. Why stay mad at me? He got everything we both dreamed of for so long." He returned to his stone perch.

Richard nodded. "Yes, but he feels like he's the only one who's had the hard work and responsibility going with those dreams. He stayed here, working the farm. That's why he resents you."

Jack laughed—a short hard laugh— before he fell back on the rock as waves of ironic laughter rolled. He turned his head.

"Richard, do you think my time with Uncle Samuel and at school were easy? They run the School of Mines and Metallurgy with military precision. We got demerits for any misstep. It's a serious atmosphere, not given to fun. The most levity I've had since I left home came during my time in Washington. Those three months after graduation held adventure. The day at Ft. Delaware and the few days I spent with Boyd's family and the friends they were visiting in Washington DC served as my only respite."

Richard lobbed a pebble at him. "Do you regret your choices?"

He turned his head. "Not about school. If Will wants someone to blame, then he'd better look in the mirror. Do you remember how Will turned so serious after Marc and Florey went to Texas to help Boyd? He changed. Alice avoided him for months and preferred me because of it. Then Uncle Samuel came for his visit. When he discovered how much I read and my high marks in school, he talked to Pa. Uncle Samuel worked as a surveyor during the war. He told Pa seeing to my education would please him as he lost his only son, my cousin, during the war. I wasn't sure, but Alice said she'd wait. I went. Once I finished all of my regular courses plus extra studies with a tutor Uncle Samuel retained to prepare me for college, I returned, but you remember what happened when I came home to visit at the end of '69?"

"You arrived to find Will and Alice engaged."

"Yes, and my reaction went beyond reason. I lit out on my own. Uncle Samuel expected me back to finalize college plans. I made it to Colorado and presented myself for the first job available with the railroad. The Irish and Chinese had most of the rail jobs, but an expert on explosives said I could help him with blasting through for a tunnel. Things went well for the first few jobs. Then one went awry. A few of their men and I became trapped after a blast. One old man and I survived. He infuriated me."

"How?"

"The old man told me to go home."

Richard laughed and threw another pebble at him. Jack knocked it away.

"You obviously didn't listen," Richard said.

"Well, not at first, but I did decide to go back to Uncle Samuel's and took the college entrance examination. I entered college in the autumn of '71."

"What the man's name?"

"Kolek, Silas Kolek. His talk about earning money so his niece could go to college stayed with me."

"Did you ever try to find him?"

"No, why would I?"

"Because he changed your life," Richard said.

Jack felt everything still inside of him. He turned his head to look at the river.

"I guess I hadn't given that much thought."

"Maybe you should."

"I bet he's dead."

"Still—," Richard said.

"I'll do some checking." Jack glanced back at his friend. "But anyway, Will made his choice, Alice made her choice, and I made mine. Each must accept the realities surrounding those choices."

Only the sound of the flowing river passed between them for the next few minutes. Jack shifted and stood, dirt and leaves crackling under his shoes.

"Just remember how I stayed mad at Marc and John for their choices not to come home right after the war. I felt they should have been here," Richard said.

"I know." Jack resumed his seat on the large rock.

"Then think of it that way." Richard sat beside him. "You felt it too."

He nodded. "But that's not the same thing. Will and I loved the same girl; something hard to watch."

"It's cost both of you enough in different ways." Richard stood and patted his shoulder. "Well, good night, Jack. Do you want me to go to town with you to meet this Cummings fellow?"

Jack shook his head. "I appreciate it, but let me meet him. You don't need to step into trouble. Besides, I need to stop by and see Will first."

Richard gave a low whistle. "If you do that, you might not make it to town."

Chapter Four

The farmhouse with the wide front porch appeared well tended. Harvested fields stretched out to the left, and a large barn stood to the right. Mina sighed as Daniel pulled the reins to halt the horses and rented buggy. He pushed back his derby hat as he turned toward her.

"Well, Mina, either he's here or never came home. This community is closed-mouthed. It makes me wonder—"

The door opened and a stocky man of average stature stepped outside, pulling the door closed behind him. He removed his hat, revealing brown hair.

"Good morning. How can I help you folks?" he said. The caution in his eyes belied the cordial tone of his voice and polite words.

Daniel shot Mina a look. She could tell her cousin didn't like the double-sided greeting. They couldn't leave now. *Oh, please, Daniel.* She bit at her fingernail. Her cousin sighed and faced the man.

"Good morning. I'm Daniel Cummings and this is

my cousin, Mina Kolek."

Blue-green eyes held them in steady regard. "Why are you here?"

Mina's anticipation trumped the men's measured mutual assessment. "We are looking for Jack Johnson. I assure you. It is nothing criminal or ill intentioned. More curiosity than anything else."

A slight smile lifted the corner of the man's mouth.

"Curiosity? That's certainly tamer than my business with Jack."

Mina frowned. What did he mean? An unexplainable protectiveness for Jack rose up in her.

"I don't understand, Mr.—"

The man looped his fingers around his suspenders. "Johnson. Will Johnson. You see, Miss Kolek, I haven't seen my brother in quite a few years, although, my mother did see him yesterday."

Daniel shook his head at her and turned to Jack's brother.

"We're sorry to have bothered you, Mr. Johnson. There's obviously unresolved family business here. We won't trouble you further. If you happen to see your brother, please give him our regards in connection with Silas Kolek." Daniel reached in his pocket, retrieving a piece of paper. "Here's our address in Colorado if he cares to contact us."

Will stepped forward to take the paper as a horse and rider appeared. He dropped his outstretched hand.

"If I'm not mistaken, he can take it from you now."

Mina turned, anticipation knotting her stomach. Tension crackled when the taller man dismounted next to them. She received a brief glance from a pair of river green eyes, accompanied by a gentleman's hat tip before both she and her cousin became spectators of the brothers' reunion.

"Jack, don't bother with apologies. I ain't—excuse me, college-man—I'm *not* accepting any. Marc's tried to convince me different, but you belonged *here*."

Jack Johnson pushed back his hat. He had short, side-parted brown hair—chestnut hair— much darker than that of the glowering brother still awaiting a reply. Mina held her breath in anticipation. What would his voice sound like? She'd imagined it—

A smooth, deep tenor voice, laced with exasperation, spit out the anticipated words. She shivered.

"Doing what, Will? I came back from the preparatory studies with Uncle Samuel to find Alice courting you. She made her choice, so I chose not to go to college, but I couldn't stay here and watch. If not for an old miner and a botched tunnel blast, I might not have returned to Missouri for the chance at college offered by our uncle. I'd still be scraping by with the Chinese and Irishmen—a right good lot, too," Jack said.

Tenderness tugged at Mina's heart. He remembered Uncle Silas. Too bad Jack's brother did not share her feelings.

Will's expression hardened. He knocked Jack to the ground without further preamble.

Mina gasped and moved, but Daniel kept her seated.

Jack rubbed his jaw, shook his head and sprang to his feet.

"I'm getting tired of such greetings. Boyd's brother, Ben, did the same thing when I met him in Washington."

Will dropped his fists. Mina held her breath.

"Did you hit him back for both of us?"

Jack grinned. Just for an instant, the men before her seemed like brothers instead of enemies.

"I sure did. He's actually a friend now."

Will grimaced and lifted his fists.

The door opened. A woman with gray-streaked brown hair emerged, followed by a pretty blonde woman slowed by the later stage of pregnancy.

"William Hockley Johnson, stop it this instant. It's time to stop feeling slighted by your brother's choice of a life away from here. Your pa tried to talk sense into you before he passed. Even when Marc and Florey gave up their life in Texas to come here, it didn't appease you. Have you ever wondered why no one else feels anger toward your brother? " The older woman glanced at the blonde woman behind her. "I don't mean this against you, Alice." Firm strides then placed her in the middle of them. "It seems to me, Jack lost the love of his youth to you. After years of indecision, she chose. You boys knew that day would come. As your mother, I expected the other one to need time away. Jack's actions made me miss him, and your actions made me proud of the husband and father you became, and grateful for your care during your father's illness and passing, but neither of you have the right to be upset with each other."

A man emerged from the side of the house. Everyone jumped a bit and turned toward him. A more mature version of Jack—tall, broad shouldered, and narrow at the hip—like the oldest brother Marcus, perhaps. Uncle Silas told her Jack idolized Marcus. They must take after their father, whereas Will resembled their mother.

"Well said, Ma. Now it's my turn." Marcus advanced with smooth agility. He gave Daniel and Mina a cursory glance. "Why don't you show these good people our customary hospitality? I'll deal with these two."

"We'll help, Marc." A redheaded man rode into the yard along with a dark-haired giant of a man.

Will turned his back on the new arrivals. "We do indeed have other visitors," he said, taking his mother by the elbow. "Ma, this is Daniel Cummings and Mina Kolek. They've come to see Jack."

Jack's startled glance found her. He stepped toward their buggy.

"Silas Kolek's niece?"

A wave of satisfaction coursed through Mina. He *did* remember her uncle. She started to get out of the buggy, but Daniel put a hand on her arm.

"Yes, sir. After what I've just witnessed, I'm not sure of allowing her to make your acquaintance," Daniel said.

Allowing? Her cousin knew better, or he should.

The older woman stepped forward. "Please don't judge us too harshly, Mr. Cummings. My husband only passed last week and Jack arrived yesterday. I'm Emily Johnson. Won't you please come in and visit? I have hot coffee and a few biscuits left."

Daniel hesitated. "Well—"

Mina put a hand on his shoulder. "Daniel, please. We've traveled a long way, and we did come unannounced."

He jumped down and turned to help her. Satisfaction filled Mina.

The blonde-haired woman advanced with

outstretched hands and smiled. "I'm Alice Johnson. Yes, please come in, Miss Kolek."

Mina returned her smile and took her hands. They walked toward the house. Alice released Mina and stopped beside her husband.

"Will Johnson, stop this foolishness." Alice's blue eyes went to her youngest brother-in-law. "Welcome home, Jack."

Mina watched for a tell-tell-look from Jack Johnson but found only a look of gratitude and family affection in his response.

"Thank you, Alice. It's good to see you."

That almost earned Jack another well-aimed punch, blocked by his oldest brother's quick reflexes.

Marc Johnson held Will's clinched fist in his palm. "Stop it, Will. John, come get him. We're not resolving this in front of women folk and guests."

Jack turned to her. "Excuse us. I will return to further your acquaintance."

Mina smiled. He had manners.

Marc advanced toward Jack, who pivoted and held up his hands in surrender. "I'll come on my own. Do you want to ride with me?"

"I did walk over," Marc said.

In a matter of minutes, the group disappeared on their horses.

Mina didn't want to move. She'd found Jack. Maybe the men could resolve things and return before they finished Mrs. Johnson's refreshments.

"He's here," Mina said.

Daniel removed his hat and shook his head at her. Mina shrugged. What else could she say? He held open the door for her.

"I'm already missing the city," he said as he followed her inside.

Chapter Five

The rushing water of the Ouachita swirled around the large rocks breaking the surface. Jack gazed at the water from his saddle for a moment before looking toward the two men restraining his irate brother. His characteristic nature of affability evaporated. After Marcus dismounted, Jack swung to the ground. He threw his hat in the dirt and shrugged out of his dress coat and vest. His eyes stayed on Will as he secured both on his saddle. The hatred in his brother's gaze, as he fought to free himself from Richard and John, ignited old grievances in Jack. He loosened his necktie.

"Will, a friendly wrestle would've served. This is not what I wanted—remember that." All thoughts of consideration left him. "Let him go."

College taught Jack discipline and his Irish friends taught him how to win a fight. The unrefined brawls of their youth had not prepared Will for the skills Jack now used.

Jack easily dodged well-aimed punches and delivered a rapid succession of blows to his brother's face and stomach as they stood toe–to-toe. Will's well-muscled, stockier frame kept him on his feet longer than most under such an onslaught. He managed one reeling punch to Jack's jaw before he staggered back and fell from a return blow.

Marcus stepped between them. Jack kept his fists and boxing stance firm until his eldest brother quirked his eyebrow. He dropped his hands and took a deep breath to slow the pounding of his heart and head.

"Get him up, boys," Marc said.

Will spit blood on the ground and rasped, "I hate you more than ever, Jack."

Reason, clarity, and sadness swirled within as Jack turned back toward the group.

"It's your choice, Will. I'll not try to meet your expectations. You have every reason for happiness in your life here. Don't use me as an excuse for the discontent you feel." He wiped away the blood on his lip with the back of his hand and retrieved his hat. "Richard, I'm going to meet with those visitors. I'll come back to your place tonight."

"I'll let Jenny know," Richard said.

Jack mounted his horse.

Will jerked away from John's hold. "Don't you go near Alice and my boy."

"Don't be ridiculous, Will. Of course, he'll visit with them and Ma," Marcus said.

Will glared at him and failed to read their older brother's face as well as Jack did.

The splash Jack heard as he rode away brought a needed smile to his bruised face.

~

A small boy ran out of the door with Alice close

behind him.

"Robert Johnson, come back here."

Jack jumped off his horse and caught his nephew before he reached the barn. The boy kicked and squirmed. He stilled for a moment when his mother grabbed him, but soon resumed his tantrum. Jack retrieved him, holding him up by the back of his shirt.

"Young man, do not kick your mother," he said.

Astonished blue-green eyes peered up at him. The lad swallowed hard once Jack placed him on the ground. He kicked at the dirt.

"Yes, sir."

Alice squatted in front of her son. She pointed toward the door.

The boy dropped his chin and nodded. He cocked his head to the side. "Uncle Jack?"

"That's me, Nephew."

The boy ran back to the house.

Jack met Alice's tired gaze. Even now, he could still see the girl he and his brother had competed for all those years. Now, she had a son.

"How old is he?"

"Four." Her eyes searched behind him. "Where's Will?"

He watched her lick her lips and remembered how such small things used to make his young heart race. He still adored her, just not in the same way. No, no guilt tremored through him for retained past affections, only for what he had to tell her now.

"I didn't kill him, but it might look like I came close—he wanted a fight, so I gave him one. It's not resolved, Alice. Darned if I know why, but I can't stay now."

Her eyes locked with his. "Your mother said you're arranging to move home."

"Yes, but Will won't forgive me. It'll cause chaos in your lives if I return."

Alice reached up to touch his bloodied lip. "Let's go get you cleaned up a bit. I'm sorry, Jack."

Jack squeezed her hand for a brief moment. He stepped back, not wanting to seem inappropriate. "As long as he's good to you, I have no regrets. We'll remain friends."

"He's a good husband and father. I love him."

"Good. I better let Ma tend me and visit with our company," he said.

"They're nice," she said.

He caught something in her voice. "What? Alice—"

She shook her head. "Nothing, come on in, Jack."

The deep pools of homesickness departed the moment he stepped into his boyhood home. The mantle over the fireplace where his father's pipe still lay, the large weathered dinner table, and the simple chairs holding his mother and their guests welcomed him.

His mother rushed to her feet. "Oh, dear—Jack, look at you." She hurried to pour water in the basin bowl on the washstand.

Alice ushered him into one of the chairs.

The small, well-dressed woman also stood.

"You're not as big as a minnow fish," he said. *Why had he said that aloud?* He cleared his throat. "No offense, ma'am."

He half expected the man in the well-tailored suit to take him outside to defend her honor. Instead, their guests burst into laughter.

"My family thinks the same, Mr. Johnson. But I'd

advise you not to misjudge her strength by her stature," the man said.

The small woman removed her gloves and rolled up her sleeves. "Daniel, I think you have a patient."

The man next to her removed his suit jacket. "I think you're right, Cousin."

He watched his mother and Alice share a smile. His ma squeezed the water from the cloth. "Jack, let me clarify your earlier introduction to these fine people. This is Dr. Daniel Cummings and his cousin, Mina Kolek. He came from Chicago to meet Miss Kolek here. You see, he will soon set up his medical practice in Denver. Mina lives there with her Uncle Silas."

Jack's eyes went from his mother to Miss Kolek. This didn't make any sense. "That's nice, but why did you meet in Malvern?"

Mina took the rag from his mother and crossed to him. Smoky blue eyes framed by dark brown eyelashes met his. "To be honest and forthright, I came to check on you." His confusion must have shown because she continued. "It does sound ludicrous. I've remained fascinated by the idea of you ever since Uncle Silas came home to recover after the tunnel blast you shared. He indulged me, thinking it would pass. However, after I wrote him a letter during my last year in college about coming here someday, he made plans. I stayed with Daniel's family, my relatives in Illinois, during school. After my return to Colorado, many things happened. Let's just say, my uncle's health would not let him fulfill his promise for this trip. So, Daniel agreed to this detour, to humor me." She sighed and bit at a fingernail.

Complete silence followed her candid words. All

eyes stayed fixed on him until he shook his head, laughing. Everyone shared looks of uncertainty until he spoke.

"Thank you, Miss Kolek, for one of the nicest stories I've ever heard. Your uncle made me so mad because he tried to send me home. It seemed impossible in my mind. So, I went to the only other home I knew— my Uncle Samuel's. Because I did, I now have a Civil Engineering degree and work as a surveyor for the railroads."

Dr. Cummings took the rag from Mina. He inspected Jack's face and checked his ribs. "I don't think you'll need my tending. How about your brother?"

Jack jerked away. "It's likely."

The door opened and Richard and John assisted a wet and bloodied Will into the house.

"Who threw this man into the river?" Dr. Cummings asked.

"I did," Marc said, closing the door.

"He'll have worse risks from bacteria there than the initial cuts," the doctor said. "Put him in the bedroom."

"Doc?" Everyone nodded. "Listen, we survived worse during the war," Marc said.

"That may well be, Mr. Johnson. But, you may not know how many died from the germs infecting their wounds rather than the actual wound damage. I'll see to him at once."

"I'm coming to help," Alice said.

His mother's eyes filled with tears. Jack stood to envelope her in a hug.

"I'm sorry, Ma. He wouldn't listen and wanted to fight. Believe me, this isn't what I wanted."

She pushed away, retrieving a cloth to dab her eyes. "I know, Jack. He's been chewing this bone for years. It breaks my heart. Your former closeness makes it harder to accept. Still, I don't want either of you hurt. He's worked hard, Jack." She patted his arm. "I'm going to help see to him."

Guilt and exasperation welled up inside him. He sank back down onto the chair and hit the top of the table with his hand.

He heard a soft gasp and turned.

"Oh, Miss Kolek, I'm so sorry for startling you. I beg your pardon, ma'am."

Her eyes darted toward the bedroom door. She started backing toward it. "Do you have trouble with your temper often, Mr. Johnson?"

"What? No—" He chuckled. "No, Miss Kolek. In fact, I don't like to carry grudges."

Confusion showed on her face. "But you left because—"

"I returned from my preparatory courses to find Alice and Will engaged. I felt heartbroken and angry with myself. If I'd never left to go with Uncle Samuel, maybe she would have picked me. Time away taught me acceptance. God's plan all along." Realization and clarity settled on him. He stood.

"Miss Kolek, I am flattered and intrigued by your journey here. Please tell your uncle how much he influenced me. It's unfortunate I have failed to meet your expectations. It's clear my brother won't accept my coming home. Therefore, I must change my plans. It's a pleasure to meet you, Miss Kolek, but I must be going." He glanced at the door on the left.

The rustling of the underskirt of her long bodice

dress as she shifted forward diverted his gaze to her. Images of fashionable porcelain dolls came to mind. He noted the indentation of her tiny waist toward the line of buttons on the jacket cut front of her garment. His eyes met hers.

Concern reflected in the blue eyes under her fashionable bangs, and her hand shook as she patted the fancy twist sweeping up her hair. She licked her lips. "But aren't you going to tell your family?"

Why did she care so much? Jack continued on his path until he reached the door. He looked back at the diminutive woman. "You amaze me, Miss Kolek. Not that it's any of your business, but I plan to retrieve my things from Richard's and stop back here on my way to the train station."

"Where will you go?"

"Please don't concern yourself." He shook his head at her imprudent persistence, flashing a sardonic smile. "Goodbye, Miss Kolek."

Once outside, Jack stopped halfway across the yard to his horse and turned toward the house one more time. This wasn't his home anymore. The loss of his father had sealed it. He'd never felt more alone.

Chapter Six

The swirling waters drew him, they babbled the song and history of the Rockport shores. He made for the scene of the fight—their favorite fishing and swimming spot, instead of Richard's. The early autumn breeze continued to hold significant warmth. Arkansas summers retained enough heat to hold cool weather at bay when the seasons began to change. He assessed the water—no stagnation or signs of mosquitoes. He'd still have to watch out for leeches though. After a moment's hesitation, he sat down and stripped off his shoes and socks. The cool river water soothed his travel-weary feet and his head.

"Dr. Cummings seems to think the river will kill ya."

He turned to find Marcus on the shore.

Jack grinned and waded a bit deeper.

"Marc, I figure we'd all be dead by now if that's true."

His brother laughed at him. "Let's find out."

Jack barely caught his breath before his brother's

equal weight and height plunged them into the rushing water. His head broke the surface to find Marc heading for their favorite rock. He swam behind him. They crawled onto the large boulder in tandem.

He slapped his brother on the foot. "Where's your boots?"

Marcus laid on the rock, shaking his wet hair out of his eyes.

"I pulled them off while watching you wade. The war taught me quietness when needed."

Jack realized they had never talked much about the war, even after Marc's delayed homecoming in the mid-autumn of 1866.

Jack pulled a leech off his brother's back and dropped it back into the water. After a cursory check of his own person for any of the pests, he stretched out beside Marc. "I visited Ft. Delaware."

Marc rolled over and sat up with his arms propped on his knees. A flash of pain flickered for a moment and his jaw tensed. "Why?"

"I found myself close enough to visit and something in me needed to understand what you went through as a prisoner of war there."

Marc's voice held no emotion. "You can't. Only John, Boyd, and the others held there do."

Jack dropped his head. "I know that now. John said the same thing last night, but the guards and officer I met did give me a little insight. You and John almost died there. Boyd made a tough decision you all had to live with. I'm sure he felt taking the oath of allegiance to the Union saved all three of you at that juncture. John and you were too incoherent and ill. He took responsibility for you. You'd have made the same decision for him if it saved his life. But more important, Marc—you lived. I'm grateful Boyd's uncle knew the right people who found him at Ft. Delaware. It gave you the opportunity to leave early because of your illness. Many soldiers never had that chance. "

"That's true." Marc sighed. "So, I assume you talked to Boyd about this during your time in Washington?"

"Yes. Were you angry?"

"At Boyd? No. Ashamed because we took the oath of allegiance early? Yes. I know God knew the timing, though. Because soon after we got to Texas, the war ended while we recuperated." Marc stroked his mustache. "But at the same time, guilt about taking the oath and Boyd's situation—his wife and son dying while he fought in the war—in Texas, served to keep John and me away for a bit." His eyes met Jack's. "Do you remember how angry Richard stayed at John and me at the end of the war?"

"That's right. He reminded me last night. When you didn't come home right away, he began hating you like Will hates me."

Marc held up a finger. "Hold on—yes, the same strong emotions, but for entirely different reasons. See, he'd soldiered beside me away from here. So, even though we fought a couple of times after we got home, our experiences in the war bound us closer than our shared childhoods."

"Marc, you've been here with Will and Alice for a few years now. Why is he so mad at me? I understand some of it but not the depth of it."

Marc leaned over to put a hand on his shoulder. "I think he views you like the prodigal son in the Bible, and he's determined no fatted calf or welcome home party are deserved. That's what he's feared, even though his view of you borders on ridiculous. It's beyond reason, but he doesn't want you acclaimed for your accomplishments while sacrificing the recognition he feels is his due—maybe he wants you to beg or something. He's not thinking straight. Now that Pa's gone, he can make certain—"

The blood drained from Jack's face, and he swallowed hard. While he understood Will's resentment to a degree, the magnitude of it now registered. "He really hates me. That's so hard to believe."

Jack shrugged off Marc's hand and lay back on the rock.

"I never took any money from Pa, Marc. He offered when I came home that one time after my regular schooling and preparatory classes ended. Uncle Samuel had refused any compensation when I first went to Missouri with him. The only period of rebellion came when I ran off to the railroad after learning Alice had accepted Will's proposal. Silas Kolek's counsel sent me back on the right path. Still, my hurt pride kept me from coming here."

"Jack, sit up and look at me." Marc waited until he complied. "How smart are you? There's book learning and life learning."

Jack scratched his head and grinned. "It's surprising, but I'm smart, to an astounding level, in the book learning. My mind soaked up all those books the professors offered. Now, life learning—that's an adventure. Thunder it all, Marc, I ain't gonna lie. It's been fun. But, I've also nearly lost my life a few times and have seen more than a few lose theirs.”

“Don’t be ashamed of the accomplishments you’ve made or the life you’ve lived. Why do you want to come home now? You need to know for yourself more than for the rest of us,” Marc said.

Jack’s heart pounded. How could he disappoint the brother he’d always wanted to be like?

“Marc, I’ve tried to walk a good path, but the longer I’m away without ties, it gets harder. I used to bypass the saloons. Now, I stop in for a drink. I used to flirt with the girls but left them pouting. It’s getting harder to do that. It’s hard to stay in church when you travel around the way I do.”

He searched his brother’s face for disappointment but only found compassion.

“Jack, I struggled with that for a time before I finally came home after the war. One more piece of advice: Don’t go up those stairs in the saloon. I never did, and I’ve never regretted it. Before I left for the war, Pa told me those choices only condition you for carnality instead of love. Also, one question: Do you think living here will fix things? I’m going to tell you right now, that’s not a certainty.”

“I know. But I’d like my family around to remind me of myself, every now and then,” Jack said.

Marc grinned. “I’d love the chance.”

“Our brother won’t allow it.”

Marc stood. He reached down to give Jack a hand. “He’s not the only one who has a say, Jack. Could you live in Hot Springs first and give him time to adjust to you again? Give him time to remember your old inseparability.”

“Yes, or I could go to Missouri or stay in Colorado

after this next job is finished. Uncle Samuel gave me an open invitation when I stopped by on my way here. We've written regularly. Why?"

"Well, I may know someone who can help us with this." Marc stroked his chin. "Do you know the name of Malvern's current mayor?"

"No, I heard they tried to move the county seat from Rockport to Malvern in February."

"Yes, that didn't succeed, but it's only a delay of the inevitable. The elections next summer will be sure it's done by autumn's end next year. Anyway, your old friend and my fellow soldier, Samuel H. Emerson, is the mayor," Marc said.

"Time does go by faster than you realize. I remember him as only about fourteen when our Rockport boys marched away to war."

"Yes, but he managed to be one of the few of our original company to make it all the way through the war to the surrender of the Confederacy at Appomattox, even with being wounded a few times. I thought he died at Gettysburg. He went down about the time John also fell wounded, but we became prisoners in that orchard. Sam and I have shared many a conversation since Florey and I returned to Arkansas. He's a good man. I want you to know things move forward whether you remain here or live away. It's God who guides us home. John and I learned that. Anyway, little brother, I think you should go finish whatever survey job you have in Colorado and talk to them about a position in Hot Springs instead of here when you finish. In the meantime, let Richard, John, and me work on talking sense into Will."

Jack hung his head and sighed. The huge boulder

under his feet seemed the only solid thing in his life. "I didn't think things would unfold this way, brother."

Marc bumped him with his shoulder. "Few things do," he said and pushed Jack into the water.

Chapter Seven

Jack stared out the train window; he wanted to deny the premature and imminent departure about to take place. The sad but resigned look on his mother's face when Marc brought her to Richard's house the previous night continued to gnaw at his gut. His goodbyes lasted longer than he anticipated due to train issues when he tried to leave the previous afternoon. The additional night at Richard's gave him more time with his mother and Marcus but only postponed the inevitable.

"Well, Mr. Johnson, it looks like you missed your planned departure yesterday. Where are you heading?"

He glanced toward the aisle. "Hello, Dr. Cummings. My ma said you did a fine job patching up my brother. How is he?" Confusion coursed through him. "And why are you not on the train to Little Rock, taking you to St. Louis today?"

"Excuse me." The man gestured toward the seat behind him. "Mina, if you please."

The small woman did not even so much as spare a glance his way as she slid into the seat behind him. Her cousin took his place beside her.

"He'll remain sore for a good while. You cracked a couple of his ribs, came close to breaking his nose, and bruised his face in quite a few places, but he will recover. You have a perplexing relationship."

Jack grunted. "True. Thank you for taking care of him."

"As to your last question, I hope to catch a colleague of mine before he completes his visit to Hot Springs. He joined me for dinner in Malvern upon my arrival last week. I sent a telegram to him this morning." Dr. Cummings met Jack's eyes as he turned. "Now I have a couple of questions. Do you think your brother has any concept of the difficulty of the schooling you completed or the job you do? And do you think you could return to farming?"

Jack tipped back his hat. He met the man's direct gaze. "No, and I don't think he wants to know. It doesn't matter to him. On the other hand, I grew up farming, but Will stepped in for Pa, and I admire the hard work he does daily. I'm not sure. It's one thing to do something as a child and another to take on all the responsibilities and risks of it as an adult."

Dr. Cummings extended his hand. "Mr. Johnson, please accept my apologies for misjudging you. I'd be pleased if you would call me Daniel."

Jack hesitated. This olive branch appeared genuine. He clasped his hand. "Thank you, Daniel. Call me Jack. Why did—"

"Your answer showed character and maturity. Two things your brother finds you void of because he's blinded by resentment," Daniel said.

Jack let out a deep breath and sat up a little

straighter. "Thank you." His eyes darted toward Mina, but she continued to stare out the window. He hoped she might reconsider her judgment. The furrow between his eyebrows deepened when she bit her bottom lip and a small frown creased her pretty forehead under her fringed bangs.

"Mina?" Daniel put a hand on his cousin's arm. "What's wrong?"

"Mr. Mathias is on the platform," she said.

"That gambler? Why does this disturb you?"

"Because, regardless of the seemingly easy convenience for him to 'keep an eye on me' for Uncle Silas. His arrival and departure mirror mine too well."

Jack glanced out the window and caught sight of the well-dressed man right before he stepped up into the train car. He knew the sort. Most women appeared charmed by their flattery, so Miss Kolek's reaction surprised him.

The gambler approached and removed his hat. "Miss Kolek, what a delight to travel in your company once again." The astute eyes moved to Dr. Cummings. "It's nice to see your beau with you this time."

Mina shifted in her seat and Jack caught the pleading look she sent his way. So, they did not want the man alerted to her traveling with her cousin. He smiled at the man.

"Yes, they make a fine looking couple. Don't they, sir?"

The keen eyes granted him grudging acknowledgement. "Indeed, and you are?"

"Jack Johnson." He tilted his head instead of offering his hand. "You see, I am the reason they came to Arkansas. Miss Kolek's uncle is an old friend, and he planned to visit me too. Unfortunately, his health prevented it. Therefore, I now find the need to visit him instead."

Mina's eyes widened for a moment. However, Daniel grinned.

"Jack, you have spoiled the surprise. I didn't tell her. We will stop in Hot Springs with you long enough for you to confirm your situation with the railroad."

"Uncle Silas will delight in seeing you again, Mr. Johnson," Mina said.

Dr. Cummings cleared his throat. "So you see, Mr. Mathias, Miss Kolek is well chaperoned for her journey. Let me once again express my gratitude to you for keeping watch over her during her trip to Arkansas."

"There is one thing puzzling me, Dr. Cummings. Since you traveled from Chicago, why did you not wait for her in St. Louis?" Mr. Mathias inquired.

Daniel's eyes narrowed. "I'll excuse the personal nature of your question this time, sir. The truth—we lacked certainty of Mr. Johnson's presence in Rockport or Malvern, or if his family still lived in the area. I wanted to ascertain those things before she came, as well as having time in Hot Springs to consult with medical colleagues. "

Jack didn't want to be involved. He had a tentative plan thanks to Marcus, but the way the man looked at Mina made the hair on his neck prickle. "Mr. Mathias, Silas Kolek is a person of great significance to me, therefore, his niece's wellbeing concerns me, also. Dr. Cummings and I will see to her care from here. Might I ask what has abbreviated your visit after such a long journey?"

Mr. Mathias's icy blue eyes met his. "Actually, my

business is in Chicago. I only continued here to see to Miss Kolek due to her uncle's concerns. I'll now go to Illinois after trying my luck in Hot Springs for a few days."

"Will you return to Denver again in the future?" Mina asked.

"That depends on my business, Miss Kolek. Well, I'll find my seat. Once again, your journey's success delights me."

Jack's eyes never left the man as he made his way to a seat at the back of the train car.

"He's no better than all the saloon and camp trash I met growing up in Colorado. He just dresses better," Mina said.

Jack's eyes widened and he turned his head in time to see a slight red flush stain her cheeks.

"Don't look so shocked, Mr. Johnson. My childhood with Uncle Silas has made me wiser than a prim city girl. One of the soiled doves in our town gave me advice before I left for school. She said, 'Remember this, honey, if a man prefers to look below your chin instead of in your eyes, walk away. That sort will enjoy the sway of your bustle more than the thoughts in your head. Leave them behind or send them to me.' I've never forgotten her words."

Dr. Daniel Cummings laughed outright. "You better catch your jaw and close your mouth, Jack. My cousin's refined appearance contrasts with her preference for untoward candor. Still"—he covered his cousin's hand with his own—"don't let that man concern you."

Mina's gaze moved back and forth from her cousin to the man now seated at the opposite end of the train car.

"Mina—"

Mina glanced at her cousin. "I won't, Daniel," she said, but her eyes strayed again.

Jack coughed twice before her blue eyes acknowledged him. He leaned forward and lowered his voice. "Miss Kolek, I have friends frequenting Denver on a regular basis. If it's agreeable with you, I'd like to have a few of them keep their eyes on Mr. Mathias, and their ears listening for any time he mentions you."

"Why? I'm sure Uncle Silas has friends willing to do the same," she said.

"Mina stop this. I'm not sure why you are so mad at Jack. You sure traveled a long way to see him," Daniel said, but lifted his hands in surrender when Mina crossed her arms and turned toward the window. He shook his head and shrugged. "Jack, we appreciate the offer, but you don't need to come to Denver if it is out of your way. We don't have to keep up the charade as Mr. Mathias might stay in Chicago."

"Don't flatter yourself too much. I only proposed a twist on my active plans. My next survey job is close to Denver. So, you see, now that I know Silas lives there, I do want to see him. There's a letter from Ft. Collins awaiting me at the depot in Hot Springs with the details of my job."

Mina's lips compressed. "I really see no reason for you to visit. I'll update my uncle, Mr. Johnson. Don't trouble yourself."

Hating him seemed catching; first Will and now her. Well, that wasn't fair, Jack had known about the rift with his brother, even if not the degree. Still, *her* feelings perplexed him. "You really don't like me. Do you, Miss Kolek? I'm afraid neither one of us made much of an impression on each other yesterday. However, I also remember your uncle irritated me all those years ago. The main difference is this: his life experiences with people and life gave his words validity. I thought on your judgements of me last night. All I can say is—you're liable to misjudge someone if you form unchangeable opinions of people based on one interaction."

She raised her eyebrow. "I might agree with you. Uncle Silas only met you one time."

Irritation sparked at her smirk. He bit his bottom lip for a moment. "Miss Kolek, go ahead and think what you like about me. What happened with my brother yesterday had nothing to do with you. I'll not apologize for your poor timing and unannounced visit. That's on you. At least your uncle looked beyond his meeting with me. He liked me in spite of my youthful bravado. His judgements, both negative and positive, are valid. You can't see past one thing."

Her mouth dropped open and her cousin started laughing.

"Jack Johnson." The conductor hurried down the aisle toward him.

Jack stood to shake the older man's hand. "Mr. Long, it's good to see you."

"I heard you came for a hometown visit. Thinking of moving back here?"

"Well, I'm still trying to decide. How is your wife?"

"Fine. She loves living in Hot Springs with me traveling so much. The active town removes the isolation she feels when I'm gone."

Jack smiled. He loved railroad people. "Wonderful.

Oh, let me introduce you to Miss Mina Kolek and Dr. Daniel Cummings. They will stop in Hot Springs before the long trip to Denver."

"You must visit the bath houses," Mr. Long said.

Daniel nodded. "I've heard people turn to them for medicinal purposes. I'd love to explore them once again — I mean, more if we have time."

Jack grinned at the physician's unease in front of his cousin.

Mr. Long tapped Jack's arm.

"Frank Madison is engineering today. I know he'd love to visit with you. I'll walk you up if your friends can do without you on the trek to Hot Springs."

Dr. Cummings inclined his head and smiled. "Of course, do go, Jack."

"Thank you, Daniel. Please excuse me, Miss Kolek."

He started whistling, adrenaline pumping in renewed excitement, as he fell into step with his old friend.

~

Mina watched them exit the car. She crossed her arms, stuck out her bottom lip, and expelled her breath. "That man perplexes me."

"Obviously," Daniel said. "Why?"

"Did you notice him transform before our eyes once his friend came? Instead of the disagreeable man that we've seen over the last couple of days, he became this light-hearted person. His entire countenance changed."

"Don't speak for my impression, Mina. My initial impression showed me two brothers confronting each other. That's why I wanted us to leave before they invited us inside. Jack's right. Our unannounced arrival came at an unfortunate time. I really didn't allow myself to form an opinion of him until you described his angry outburst. That's why I sought more information today. I think the man we witnessed today represents the one he has become during these years away. The other resulted from the homecoming thwarted by his brother's hand; guilt and remorse felt more deeply because of family. Rejection seems never so bitter than at home, or former home places."

"Aren't you the philosopher?" Mina stared at her cousin in disbelief. "How did you ever come to make such incredible deductions?"

Daniel's face grew somber. "How many deep conversations have you had with my mother about Uncle Silas? Or even better, have you ever asked the man who raised you about his experiences with family?"

"Some, but he won't tell me everything. I never considered applying those things to Mr. Johnson." Mina's eyes widened. "That's it. That's why he told Mr. Johnson to go home all those years ago—to avoid his fate."

Daniel met her eyes. "Something like that. You know—I think Uncle Silas may be of benefit to Jack a second time."

Mina bit the edge of her fingernail. "Maybe, but he's not what *I* expected."

Wry amusement tinged Daniel's words. "Poor Jack. He has no idea how to actualize the man your years of pondering created. Why don't you give him a chance to show you his true self?"

"What do you mean?"

"You see, my dear cousin, I had no expectations.

So, my opinion of him comes from experience alone. My initial quick judgements from the unfortunate circumstances of our first meeting are easier for me to rescind. He's someone who could easily become a friend. I like him."

Mina bit at her thumbnail. If only, Jack— no, she couldn't make him different. She stared out the window. "I'm not sure."

"At least there's one thing you like about him," Daniel said.

She turned to look at him. "What?"

"The man seems to like looking you in the eye when he talks."

Mina's cheeks flushed. Daniel laughed. The train shuddered into motion.

Chapter Eight

"Mina, do try to keep your amazement less apparent," Daniel said.

Mina's wide eyes swept the luxurious lobby of the Arlington Hotel. She composed herself while Daniel finished registering them. This place held the stature of places in bigger cities. She bit her bottom lip and hoped the room arrangements for the night did not overextend her cousin's means.

The outside of the grand establishment rivaled anything she had seen before, even in Chicago. Although Daniel withheld his agreement, she maintained her opinion. Seeing the interior of this still young hotel left no doubt for her.

Jack laughed and shook his head when Daniel told him where they planned to stay. Then he shrugged. "A spectacular hotel choice. They finished in '75, and it is the largest in Arkansas. Mr. Reynolds offered me a night there when I stopped by on my way home, but I declined. I'd rather stay with a friend. When you travel like I do, accommodations within a private home seem more of a luxury than what others find luxurious."

Mina remembered her surprise at his comment and later, her shock at his jovial demeanor when his friend met him on the platform. The man's behavior stupefied her.

Daniel took her elbow, while she took care to mind the small ruffled train extending from the underskirt of her dress, as they followed the boy leading them to their rooms. Her mind continued to race with conflicting thoughts.

Her cousin turned to her after the boy unlocked the door next to hers. "Refresh yourself, Mina. We will go find sustenance when you're ready. I'd like to further investigate the popular bath houses this afternoon."

Mina laughed. "If you don't mind, an outside view suffices for me."

He sighed. "There are many medicinal advantages to them. I must admit to going inside one the last time I visited here. Remember, I attended the big medical meeting here this past April. Many enjoy the baths."

"I'm sure. Still, I'd prefer to refrain if you don't mind. There must be other things to see."

"Yes, this mountain town has many sights. I did not get to investigate as much as I'd have liked during the day I spent here on my way. My colleague took up most of my time."

Once again, Mina laughed. "Daniel, this does not even resemble a mountain town compared to Denver. What I see are hills; pretty hills I'd like to investigate." She stepped into her room and shut the door.

She re-emerged a few minutes later to find Daniel waiting in the hall.

After enjoying a delicious meal, they walked out of

the dining room, and a well-dressed man approached them with his hand extended.

"Dr. Cummings, the desk notified me of your arrival."

"Dr. Franklin, I'm glad we returned in time to see you again. Please meet my cousin, Miss Mina Kolek. Mina, I am pleased to present Dr. Michael Franklin, one of my old classmates."

The man's smile triggered Mina's memory. "Dr. Franklin, I believe I met you as a dinner guest at my aunt's home one evening."

His smile broadened. "How kind of you to remember, Miss Kolek. Daniel lacked certainty of your recollection of meeting me during your college days in Chicago."

Mina remembered a young man with the same smile who turned red each time she caught him watching her during the meal. She stilled her twitching lips and silenced a giggle, turning a gracious smile on the now refined physician.

"It's nice to see you again, Dr. Franklin. I understand you married a young lady from Arkansas and came here for a medical meeting."

Her astute gaze caught the fleeting look of relief on his face. No, she would never speak of the man's former admiration of her.

"Yes, that's correct. We live in Little Rock. I would delight in introducing you to Sarah someday. Perhaps on another visit? For now, might I ask to steal away your cousin for the afternoon? Dr. Keller, one of Hot Springs prominent physicians, has agreed to Daniel taking part in our medical discussion today."

Her cousin's eyes brightened.

She inclined her head. "But of course, Dr. Franklin. I—" Out of the corner of her eye, she caught sight of the lithe form of Jack Johnson striding toward them. "I believe Mr. Johnson can direct me to some local sights."

Daniel raised an eyebrow, made introductions again, and within a matter of minutes, Mina and Jack watched the two doctors depart.

"So, what do you suggest, Mr. Johnson?"

His green eyes sparkled down at her.

"Well, as I came here to determine your plans before going to the courthouse, I'll ask you to accompany me. I'd like to explore all the changes in this growing town with you."

Mina bit her lip. A man must have a trustworthy character. Each time she interacted with him made her doubt his. "Courthouse? Are you in trouble?"

"You have such an interesting opinion of me," Jack said and laughed. "No, it's a potential work situation, doing survey work for the county land office. After my meeting with my associates at the railroad about changing my position from Malvern to here, they suggested this option in this area as another possibility once I return from Denver."

Mina stared at him. His ever-changing demeanor continued to baffle her.

"If you're sure it won't be an imposition."

He offered his arm. "Not at all, Miss Kolek."

She bent her head to hide the flushed smile forming on her face. They left the extravagant hotel behind.

A few hours later, after a tedious wait at the courthouse and some precarious moments avoiding the buggies and street-railed transportation in the middle of the wide thoroughfare in front of the bathhouses, Mina felt able to breathe again. The mountain and valley views from where they stood above the town surprised her.

"The trees are so numerous. It's breathtaking, I must admit. Still—"

Jack gasped and staggered as if she had stabbed him in the heart.

"What?" she asked.

"Why did I know a pure compliment of my state's vistas would not pass without a qualification?"

He doffed his derby hat and sat on one of the rocks overlooking the panorama, turning to face her. She turned away from the view, removed her hat, and found a seat beside him.

"Surely, you must admit this differs from the mountain views in Colorado," she said.

Jack crossed his arms over his chest and shrugged. "*This* is home to me, and *that* is home to you. It's perspective. Your uncle told me you loved the mountains."

Tears misted her gaze and choked her voice. "I do." She stood. Walking a few feet away, guilt flooded her.

His voice softened. "Miss Kolek?"

"I shouldn't have come to Arkansas. My uncle lies ill in Denver. Daniel needs to be there, tending him."

"Then why did you?"

She whirled to face him, a burst of inexplicable anger flooding her. "I don't know—a silly girlhood compulsion about you. Mr. Johnson, I recognize the childish nature of this trip and beg your forgiveness. For the first time, I have absolute clarity. You need to go back to Rockport, regardless of your brother's objections. I need to go back to Denver. Daniel can assure my safety."

He gave her a scrutinizing perusal. She took a step toward him.

"Mr. Johnson, I don't want to continue to the new tower. This town of ailing tourists coming for cures irritates me. My cousin may find it fascinating, but I find it suffocating."

He remained seated, watching her with absolute calm. A gust of wind buffeted her skirt and lifted their hats from the rock. Jack retrieved their hats and tilted his face to the breeze. She wanted to scream.

"Well, if you refuse to see me back to the hotel, I'll go alone. I may look like a city girl, but Uncle Silas taught me to take care of myself in the real mountains."

Mina attempted to grab her hat from him. His emerald gaze challenged her.

She put both hands on her hips. "Give me my hat, sir."

One deft move lifted the hat high above his head. He stood there with an eyebrow quirked at her. "Only after you answer one question to my satisfaction," he said. Jack donned his hat with one hand and continued to dangle hers from the other when she didn't respond. "After all, I never asked for this visit."

His words hit Mina like a bucket of icy mountain water.

She sputtered, "Well, I . . . well, I . . ."

He dropped his hand and examined the ribbons on her hat for a moment, waiting.

"I'll answer your question," she said.

"What did Silas tell you about me that kept you so fascinated? I mean—I don't care to re-visit the rebellious, stubborn youth he met long ago. And, from your reaction to my behavior with my brother—which contained shades of me as that obstinate young man— my boyish self would find no merit in your view either."

Everything slowed within her. She lifted her eyes to meet his.

"No, not your rebellion so much—although, I found it quite adventurous at the time," she paused, unable to keep from sending him a small smile before continuing. "It became a cumulative curiosity. Did you go home? Did you continue with the railroad? Did the call home or the one to adventure win?"

He smiled and rocked back on his heels a few times before responding. "As you now know, a compromise of the two won. Still, that curiosity isn't enough to hold more than a fleeting interest in someone."

Irritation rose within her at the teasing spark in his eye. *No, she couldn't let him push her to admit more. Could she?* She clasped her hands behind her back and took two casual steps toward him, lifting her gaze to meet his at as close proximity as she dared. It took effort, but she kept her voice soft and southern sweet like her school friend from Georgia. "Please don't let my interest or actions overwhelm your male pride and ego. I can assure you, you should in no way take my interest personally." She heaved a sigh and rolled her eyes, allowing her vocal accent to return to the Illinois influence of her relatives. "If you must know, my uncle is a bit of an unlikely poet. For all his rough exterior, he has a romantic heart. I guess he passed part of it to me. *Maybe,* I came to help him finish the unfinished poem about the boy in the tunnel. It's open-ended. Now, I can help him complete the last refrain."

Jack extended her hat, watched as she adjusted it on her head, and offered his arm with a self-deprecating smile. "Shall we go?"

She took his arm, blinking a bit. *Why had she minimized the reason for her visit?*

Neither spoke until they reached the Arlington.

Outside of the entrance, he turned toward her. "Thank you for a clarifying afternoon. It's nice to provide the concluding refrain you've sought. Unfortunately, I do have work remaining in an area close to Denver, but I'll try not to trouble *you* further. I do still hope to call on Silas while in Colorado. At the conclusion of my work, I'll make my decision about my life. Good-day, Miss Kolek."

When something is no longer a pursuit and finds resolution, a sense of desolation descends. It found her at that moment.

"Mr. Johnson, where are you going?"

"As I've made all the needed arrangements, and we have concluded our visit, I plan to meet my friend, a railroad ticket agent here, and get a drink," Jack said.

"You drink?"

A smirk formed on his handsome face. "Not on a regular basis, but on occasion."

Mina glanced away as one man walked by them. Her cheeks burned. Had he overheard them? Still, she had to forge ahead. She leaned toward Jack and whispered, "Do you frequent saloons and women on occasion as well?"

The shock on his face preceded the narrowing of his eyes. "Miss Kolek, I have never heard such a brazen question from a lady's mouth. A gentleman does not discuss such matters."

"As you obviously do, may I ask if you've fallen ill before?"

Jack took her arm and led her to a secluded place beside one of the columns on the hotel porch.

"Miss Kolek, I do *not* plan on having this discussion. I will say, I know two former soiled doves—as friends only—now well established ladies within their communities—who would never put a man in the potentially embarrassing position in which you've placed me. Are you so judgmental?"

Mina placed her hands to her reddened cheeks and shut her eyes for a moment before forging ahead. "No—Yes, Mr. Johnson, I guess so, but not in the way you mean. It's been my experience to see men take advantage of women in unfortunate circumstances in the mining camps as a child. While in college, I found the differential treatment of intelligent women compared to intelligent men vast and demeaning. I must say, some women are as ruthless as men are. I'm only expressing concern for your health and that of any young lady you might plan to marry one day." She stopped, not wanting to elaborate on Sally's tragedy. It hurt too much. Still, she wanted Jack to understand. "I had a good friend at school whose fiancé frequented those places without telling her. They married; he received private treatment, she got sick, almost died, and now can never have children. In addition, she now detests her husband. They're trapped within a lifetime of unhappiness. I, for one—if I marry—will assure his past, and will have my cousin examine him before our wedding."

Jack opened his mouth and then closed it. He turned

to go, hesitated, and turned back to her. "You have no right, and may the Good Lord help your future husband. I consider myself a gentleman, most of the time, and as your convoluted concern touches me, I'll allay your fears in the most dignified manner. My feet have not climbed saloon stairs with the doves working there. Good day, Miss Kolek."

Mina chewed at a nail and watched him leave before finding a seat in one of the lovely chairs by the entrance. Her eyes took in the bustling resort town. The wind caressed her face while her mind replayed her time with Jack today—his handsome face and teasing company on the mountain. She put her hands to her cheeks. *How could she have said those things to him?* The reality of their short acquaintance made her shame worse. After all, even though she viewed him like family, thanks to all her years of girlish dreaming, they'd only met the previous day. A sigh of bewildered regret passed through her lips. She wanted to go home.

Chapter Nine

Jack punched his pillow one last time.

"Jack, will you please get still," Harold said. "I need to get up in an hour."

"Sorry," Jack muttered.

His friend released a loud breath before turning over to face him.

"I don't know what that woman said to you, but it sure ruined our evening. I even threw an extra two bits on the bar for you a drink. You still refused to have one. Not even one; after you dragged me in there."

Jack grunted. "She travels clear across the country to find me—not to meet me but to give her uncle's poem an ending. I could accept that, but then she disparages me and tries to tell me how to live."

His friend sat up laughing. "That's enough to hurt any man's pride. But it's not the first part bothering you so much. No, you aren't one to take offense easy. It's the second part. You've never liked others telling you how to live."

Jack scowled. "I don't know why that gets in my

craw. Unsolicited advice always bothers me, but I don't mind considering it once I'm alone. It's not so much the advice she gave, it's the kind of advice, and that she said it at all."

His friend raised an eyebrow. "Continue. Wait—is she pretty?"

"Not that it matters given her appalling words, but yes, she is. Still, I don't think a woman should advise a man on women matters."

Harold threw the covers off his legs and laughed. "Marry her, Jack."

Jack sat straight up in the bed. "What? Never, *ever*. She doesn't even like me."

His friend threw a pillow at him. "Get dressed, and we'll walk to the station together."

~

Jack's normal frenetic energy returned once he found a fellow surveyor traveling on their route. They talked all the way to St. Louis. He shoved all thoughts of Miss Kolek and Dr. Cummings into his peripheral interest, as well as vision. They sat across the aisle from him.

The train shuddered to a stop in a swirl of white from the smoke stack and the shrill, hollow sound of the whistle. Outside the window, he spotted two familiar profiles.

"I don't believe it," he said, smiling.

As soon as the train stilled, he hurried into the aisle, tapping each person who happened to mill in front of him.

"Excuse me, excuse me."

He bounded down the steps and onto the platform, running to catch the couple moving farther along the platform.

"Eddie Rigby!"

The stocky-framed man turned, green eyes searching. A smile erupted on the man's face as he extended his hand. "Jack Johnson. What are you doing in St. Louis?"

Jack shook hands, glancing at the lovely, dark-haired woman at the man's side. Warm brown eyes accentuated the welcoming smile.

He removed his hat.

"Miss Hallie, I mean, Mrs. Rigby."

Her rich unabashed laugh caused others to turn. Her husband smiled at her.

"Jack, you have my permission to call me Hallie. In fact, I prefer it. How are you?"

An unfamiliar lump formed in his throat. His eyes misted, and he took a moment before finding his accustomed smile.

"I get by, Hallie. But, look at you." He took her hands and assessed her stylish dress and hat. "Congratulations on your marriage. I would have loved to work with Eddie, but I think he chose a better life."

Hallie's astute eyes caught his. He squirmed under her scrutiny. "Thank you, Jack. I'm not sorry to deprive you of him. Now, enough of these niceties—what's happened?"

Jack dropped her hands, looking down. *Hold it together.* He took a couple of breaths before raising his eyes to meet hers. "My pa just died. I went home a few days ago and discovered his recent passing."

Eddie put a hand on his shoulder. "I'm sorry, my friend. We enjoyed meeting him, as well as the rest of your fine family when we stopped by on our way back from Texas this past summer. He was a good man. I think you and Marc got your sense of adventure from him.”

A sad smile formed. A lump of emotion choked his voice. “You’re right. We did.” He dropped his head and felt Eddie squeeze his shoulder. Resolve raised his head and he cleared his throat. “Thank you, Eddie. I waited too long.” Moisture misted his eyes. He blinked and averted his gaze for another moment before facing his friends again. “Anyway, I’m on my way to Denver for a survey job in the Fort Collins area.”

Hallie reached for his hands again. “Jack, timing’s not always the way we want it. It’s an illusion to think it’s *ours* to control. Only God knows in reality. There’s purpose.” She dropped his hands, stepping in for one more hug before stepping back beside Eddie. “Anyway, we’re here on business with the museum. We start home today.”

“Are you working with Madame Rousseau and Eddie or still nursing?” he asked.

A deep voice from behind him prevented her response. “Nursing? Are you a nurse?”

Hallie hesitated and smiled. “Yes, Mr.—”

“Dr. Cummings.”

Jack turned to make introductions. Daniel and Mina stepped forward.

“Dr. Daniel Cummings, please meet Mr. and Mrs. Edward Rigby of Washington D.C.”

Daniel removed his hat, shook Eddie’s hand and inclined his head to Hallie.

“It is nice to make your acquaintance. May I present my cousin, Miss Mina Kolek of Denver. I am from Chicago but traveling to Denver to establish my medical practice there."

Hallie smiled at Mina. "Miss Kolek." Her gaze moved back to the doctor. "Yes, Dr. Cummings, I nurse at St. Elizabeth's Hospital and also co-founded Hallie's House for women in difficult circumstances in Georgetown—the one near Washington D.C., not the one in Colorado. I accompany my husband and his mother on two trips to art museums throughout the year. His mother is Madame Marta Rousseau. If you know of her late husband Monsieur Rousseau—"

Daniel cut her off, "Yes, her late husband's legacy among art dealers and those in the shipping business is well known."

Eddie removed his hat, revealing curly blond hair as he nodded at Mina.

"Miss Kolek, it is nice to meet you, as well as your cousin. May I ask how you know Mr. Johnson?"

Jack turned to find Mina's eyes resting on him, so he answered for her. "I met her uncle years ago, when I first left home. They planned a trip to Rockport, but he became ill, so Dr. Cummings accompanied her instead. Now, I am traveling with them and will look in on Mr. Kolek before I start my next assignment."

Eddie and Hallie exchanged a look.

The conductor's voice called out behind Jack.

"Well, our train is ready to board. Dr. Cummings, Miss Kolek, once again, it's a pleasure to make your acquaintance. Keep an eye on our dear friend," Eddie said.

"I've tried. He doesn't seem to take advice well," Mina said.

Irritation stirred within Jack. He scowled. This drew another resounding laugh from Hallie, who took Mina's hand.

"It's a pity we do not have much time, Miss Kolek."

Mina nodded. "Maybe another time, Mrs. Rigby."

Eddie leaned in and whispered in his ear. "Tread carefully with this one, my friend. I want a letter."

Hallie stepped forward and hugged him before accompanying her husband to the train.

He heard Daniel sigh and turned.

"What?"

"It's a pity they had to leave. Our train doesn't depart for an hour. I would have loved to visit with Mrs. Rigby. Do you know where she trained?"

Jack smiled. "She has a convoluted history of which I'm sure your cousin would disapprove. However, she trained with an army doctor in Indian Territory, then in Washington, and later at the Hospital for Women and Children in Boston with Dr. Dimock."

"Dr. Susan Dimock? My, my—her death saddened the medical community. Still so young. Now, I'm even more upset. May I ask how you know the Rigbys?"

"It's complicated, but suffice it to say, we met through friends of my brother Marcus."

Mina frowned.

"Why do you think I wouldn't approve of her past, Mr. Johnson?"

Jack felt a bit smug. "Of course, I didn't meet her until after she and her late husband, James Hawkins, established Hallie's House. But, before she came to the fort in Indian Territory to work as his nurse, she worked in a saloon in Texas as a soiled dove."

Daniel straightened. "Jack, I don't think that's something to discuss with my cousin."

Jack nodded, giving Mina a satisfied look. "Under

normal circumstances, I couldn't agree more, Daniel. However, since your cousin chose to discuss such a topic with me last evening, I felt it might interest her."

Shock turned to humor as the truth of it appeared on his cousin's face. Daniel laughed outright. "Mina, you never stop astounding me. I guess it all comes from your interesting upbringing."

"I resent that." Mina's eyes flashed. "I loved my childhood with Uncle Silas. Although, I enjoyed my college time in Chicago, I wouldn't have grown-up there for anything. Uncle Silas taught me the truth about life by letting me see the true nature of people."

Jack laughed. "I'd agree your uncle appears astute, but—" He shook his head and walked away a few paces. Enough—let her judge him. At least her cousin found him tolerable. His hand felt in his pocket for his father's letter. Determination filled him. He turned.

"Daniel, I want to wish you luck on your new practice in Denver. Once I conclude my business, I might stop by to see you. Please give my best to Silas. I'd love to see him, but given his niece's disdain for me, I think it's best for us to part ways here. Anyway, I plan on riding with the engineer on this next train." He forced himself to look at Mina. "Miss Kolek, I beg your pardon for your wasted time, money, and disillusionment on my behalf. I'd like to compensate you for your tickets, so if you'll give the address to the porter on the train, he'll bring it to me."

Her blue eyes blinked, and her face paled. Why did she look so devastated?

"That's not necessary, Mr. Johnson," Mina said, placing a hand on her cousin's arm.

Daniel covered his cousin's hand and tucked it in

his arm. A polite smile appeared on the doctor's face. "No, Jack, it's not. I gained knowledge during my meeting with colleagues in Hot Springs and enjoyed seeing a bit of the country with my cousin. I'll send your regards to Uncle Silas, but please stop to see him if time allows."

Jack nodded and started to turn.

Daniel touched his arm. "Wait, Jack, one more thing, do you know the address for Hallie's House? I'd like to correspond with Mrs. Rigby. She might know a trained nurse looking for a work situation."

After promising to get him the address by the end of the journey, a pang of guilt rushed through Jack, followed by relief as he turned toward the train. He felt free again. A whistle trilled through his lips and his customary jaunt returned to his steps.

The words from his father's letter replayed in his mind and provided permission to look forward.

Chapter Ten

Mina rushed into the dry goods store, removing her hat in a flurry of ribbons.

"I apologize for being late, Mrs. Cosgrove. Daniel stayed out on a call all night, and I had to tend the scrapes from some street fights coming to our door in the middle of the night. Uncle Silas is right behind me."

The older woman patted Mina's hand. "That's fine, my dear. It's a bit slow this Monday morning."

Her uncle shuffled in after her, reaching for a cover apron.

"Good morning, Miriam."

"Good morning, Silas. Are you re-thinking living over your nephew's medical practice?"

Silas slipped on the apron and tied it. He grunted, scratching his bearded face. "Some evenings, I do. It's hard to get an uninterrupted night's sleep, but worth it at my age. The boy's a good doctor and turned my condition around when he arrived here."

The store's co-owner smiled. "He did indeed. I'm glad we are still able to run the business together. I don't know what I would have done without you after my dear husband's death, my friend. Age will never keep you from working, Silas Kolek." Her eyes went to the door. "Excuse me. Here's Mrs. Richmond."

She hurried away.

Mina continued to the back office where the ledgers waited for her. She sighed, thinking about the last couple of months. Sharing the mountains with Daniel, showing him the old cabin where Silas raised her, and helping establish his medical practice brought Mina peace for the first time since finishing college.

Following their arrival, her uncle's reaction to the update about Jack surprised her. He'd chuckled and nodded. She asked if he finished the poem a few weeks later, and he gave a vague nod but refused to show it to her. She glanced at the calendar on her desk—over halfway into November, and he still hadn't shown it to her.

Part of her felt satisfied to bring closure to the mystery of the long pondered Mr. Johnson, and she supposed her disillusionment would fade in time. It proved you should never build up people in your mind. In all fairness to Jack, the fault did not lie with him. The boy of her youthful dreams did not exist. She acknowledged her error in trying to hold him accountable.

Mina opened the ink well, dipped the pen tip, and entered the totals from the previous day's sales in the ledger. The rows of numbers kept her mind occupied until she completed her task. A sigh escaped. She added a few more bite marks to the end of her pen.

Why didn't he stop by to see Uncle Silas?

She tapped the toes of her shoes on the floor under

her desk, while continuing to ponder about Jack. Once he separated from them on the train, she never encountered him again.

Insufferable lout.

A knock on the door made her turn her head. "Yes?"

"Are the ledgers ready for the day?"

She rose, smiling. "Yes, ma'am. Here you go, Mrs. Cosgrove."

"Thank you, dear. Oh, your cousin needs to see you."

Mina frowned.

Daniel appeared in the doorway wearing a smile.

She pursed her lips. Her mind ran through the events of the busy morning. "Daniel, did I forget something at home?"

"No, no, but I forgot to tell you about my plans for today." A mixed expression of sheepishness and gaiety crossed his face. "I'm leaving for Ft. Collins this morning."

Irritation constricted her chest. She stood and moved to stand in front of him. "Ft. Collins? Today? Why didn't you tell me? I can't watch your practice today. What if there's an emergency? When will you return?"

He placed his hands on her shoulders, looking down at her with a tolerant smile. "Mina, old Dr. Brooks is at the office. He handled things before I arrived here and still has practicing rights at the hospital. The trip will only involve a couple of days by train, including the time needed to complete my business there. Uncle Silas knows, and there's no trouble in town at present—besides those sharing in your views on temperance and woman suffrage rights—so you should be fine." He ducked as she swatted at him. He laughed and continued. "All is arranged for while I'm away."

"Well, Miss Stone's views do hold merit. They may not give us the right yet, but you'll see, it's coming before the turn of the century."

He gave her an affectionate smile. "I hold it may be longer, but I'm sure you're right. May the Good Lord help us. Anyway, don't worry. I'll see you soon."

She contemplated what a greenhorn Daniel remained concerning many things in their local community.

"Be careful and stay warm."

He kissed her cheek. "I will."

She followed his hurried exit and found herself standing by the main counter in the mercantile. A comforting arm from Mrs. Cosgrove squeezed her for a moment.

"What a fine young man—the Lord blessed you and Silas when Dr. Cummings came. From what he said, things may even get easier for you, my dear."

Mina blinked. "Why?"

The woman's hazel eyes sparkled. "*Well*, he said his trip might result in a nurse for his practice."

Uncle Silas joined them. He shook his finger at his friend. "Miriam Cosgrove, he wanted to surprise her."

The woman wrinkled her nose. "Then he shouldn't have told me," she said over her shoulder as she hurried to the incoming customer.

Mina crossed her arms. "How did he find a nurse in Fort Collins? Is she trained?"

Uncle Silas propped the broom next to the closest shelf and took her arm. Once they stood inside the office, he turned her to face him.

"Mina, I love you dearly, but you must give people the chance to make their own decisions."

She nibbled at a bothersome fingernail. "I don't want bad decisions."

He chuckled. "Just because someone else decides, doesn't make their choice in error. Going to college sure changed you."

Hurt and contrition coursed through her.

"It did only in the education I received—about books, people, and my own mind. Uncle Silas, you brought me up quick, working away as you did. I enjoyed going with you, until you wouldn't let me."

"Mina, as we've discussed, things changed after your eleventh birthday. I dressed you as a boy so no one would notice, but those rough men—"

"I know, Uncle Silas, and Mr. and Mrs. Cosgrove took care of me quite well once you traveled on your own. But I liked our early years traveling together and the late winters in the cabin best. Still, you left me in town to keep from worrying about me, but I started worrying about *you* when I couldn't go with you. After that, I started anticipating potential problems and solutions for you, as well as the Cosgroves. I guess it's spread to anyone I care about. "

"I have lived a long time—I was in my fifties when you came to live with me at the age of five—and I've made plenty of bad decisions, but they're mine, and I'm still here."

Mina dropped her eyes, feeling like a child again. "Yes, sir."

He lifted her chin with an aged finger. "Caring and controlling become a two-edged sword if combined.

Jack and I prefer the first."

Mina's stomach flipped, and she placed a hand to it. She stepped back. "Why mention *him*? If he cared so much, he'd have visited you by now."

He lifted his hands. "There you go again. He's working. He paid for a boy to bring me a note the day after you arrived, and I received a telegram from him last week."

Her fists tightened, and an inadvertent foot stomp stirred the bottom of her dress.

After a long silence, during which she counted every item in the room to avoid meeting his unblinking eyes, her uncle released a deep sigh.

"Mina Jean Kolek, this town is growing faster than the wind gusting from the mountains. You can't control it any more than the chill of that breeze. Think about it. I've got to tend the store."

After he left, Mina buried herself in the month's accounts and reviewed changes in the laws. Things became more complicated when Colorado moved from being a territory and finally became an official state the previous summer.

The town now felt almost suffocated by the number of people milling about the streets. The presence of many well-known, long-standing residents remained the one good thing.

The rest did not mean much to her. Area miners came and went throughout the years. She did not have the inclination to cotton to those relocating from the rest of the states.

She searched her desk for the theatre notice from her childhood friend. Frank always made her laugh. But she'd never consider him as a potential beau.

Still, having Frank here again thrilled her. Due to his father's illness, he came to stay through the winter. His role in tonight's festivities dealt more in the care and technical aspects of the theatre than performance. The anticipation of the two-night concert opportunities with a soprano and contralto at Turner Hall caused a ripple of excitement to many. She found the newspaper notice and confirmed the time before returning to work.

Anticipation filled her at the thought of the evening outing. She loved the continual fall of temperatures from October to winter's end. She loved lingering to feel the crisp air on her face. Her uncle laughed at her. Instead of running indoors from the frost and snow, she embraced them.

Anticipation quickened her pulse as she allowed figures for sales, orders, and freight to consume her attention for the next few hours. She waved Uncle Silas away when he asked if she wanted to stop for a bite to eat. Without a break, she could leave an hour early and dress for the evening.

~

The beautiful voices of Clara Louise Kellogg and Annie Louise Cary enraptured the audience. The last note of the final selection for the evening hung in the awed air of absolute silence before the patrons joined in thunderous applause, Mina among them. A flourish of curtsies and bows, while flowers flew onto the stage, ensued with the performers and musicians basking in the accolades. She loved the encores.

The elegant crowd milled up the aisles and into the lobby where Mina waited for Frank to finish his duties. A half-hour later, her old childhood friend rushed to take her outstretched hands. She must say, outside of

Daniel and Uncle Silas; she held a singular trust for Frank. Her closest friends, besides Frank, included her cousin in Chicago, and Betsy Singer. She felt blessed to have Betsy in Denver. All the other girls educated in the secluded one room of the church-schoolhouse in their old mountain community scattered as the years passed. Betsy planned to come with her tonight, but cancelled due to a terrible cold.

"Mina, let me look at you. Well, you haven't gotten any bigger, but you sure have added refinement."

Mina twirled and finished with an exaggerated preen, patting her hair. She dissolved into giggles.

"My aunt helped guide me during my time in Chicago, not Uncle Silas," she said.

Frank laughed. He wrinkled his nose. "No, no—I remember you wearing dresses way too big or even pants, at times, to school. Of course, with the combination of the war years and frontier conditions, I'm grateful for what we did have. If Mrs. Lyles hadn't agreed to become the teacher, we wouldn't have had any schooling."

Mina pursed her lips in thoughtful contemplation. "You know, I've thought about those things. She was young and her rough husband disapproved. They said he froze to death while out trapping, but he'd brought her west from Virginia. I don't know—" She caught Frank's sparkling eyes, crossed arms, and twitching lips. "What?"

Frank held out her coat. "I think you still think too much about the secret plight—men trying to take advantage—of women."

Mina adjusted her kid gloves and slid her arms into the large sleeves of the long black cloak. "Why shouldn't I? You know the things we witnessed. The way the hold-over gold miners, and later the silver miners treated women. I can't prove it, but I think they snatched more girls and women than the Indians. And, I know widowed women not faring well when unable to return to their families."

"I won't deny that, and the lovely ladies of the evening, soiled doves, prostitutes, or, as the crude men call them—whores—abound everywhere." Frank sighed. "Still, Mina, many have chosen their way of life. You can champion for those mistreated but don't overlook the others. Plenty of well-treated females also live in these parts. Some, so much so, that they've become too uppity."

Mina whirled around to face him, lifting her eyebrow. "For example?"

"Your precious Miss Stone or, as she's wed; I would think she might allow herself the title of Mrs. Blackwell. She doesn't live here, but she wants women in this state, as well as the rest of the states, to vote."

"Frank, women are just as capable of political thought as men. Those in our neighboring Wyoming Territory agree with me. I think it depends on how informed the voter is on the issues and candidates set before them."

"Now, wait a minute, Mina. I think women have the capacity to vote well. It's the possible repercussions bothering me. For all your anger about men who don't take care of women, the results of what this suffrage movement has initiated might make it worse. Some women might even feel insulted if a man even tried to serve as their provider, protector, or defender. In my humble opinion, it verges on two-sided weaponry, and in generations to come, might cause terrible havoc.”

“You sound like all the preachers around here.” Mina bit her lip in consternation.

Frank put on his hat with a flourish. He wiggled his eyebrows. “I’m too scandalous to be a preacher.”

Mina giggled and took his arm. He held the door for her.

The frosty air stung Mina’s cheeks upon stepping into the night. The clean smell filled her nostrils. “We might get an early snow. Where will you go from here, Frank?”

“Well, I still mourn the fire in the old theatre. I’ve been with the same troupe most of my time away from here. We spent time in Montana and hope to come back here someday. Once my father recovers, I’ll find where they are and join them.”

Mina guided him to her buggy. “Mrs. Cosgrove insisted we use this tonight. The town‘s crowded state makes her apprehensive for me to walk alone. Uncle Silas agreed.”

Frank nodded. “As do I. Here let me help you up and see you home. Do you have a cup of coffee for me there?”

“Of course I do.”

They passed a couple of saloons. Noise and light spilled from the windows and swinging doors. Mina sighed once the sign for Daniel’s office came into view.

“Do you like living above a medical practice?”

“Yes, I do. It’s comforting in a way and sleep stealing in another. I—” a movement rippled the shadow of the doorway. She laid a hand on Frank’s arm. “Something’s by the door.”

“Maybe it’s a patient.”

"Maybe. Still, use caution." Mina felt for her small handbag and loosed the satin cords for access to the small Derringer pistol inside.

"I can still fight, but I've grown too vain to enjoy it. Let's hope it's a patient," Frank said.

Mina said a silent prayer of thanks for the lamp Daniel installed by the steps leading up to their door.

The person in the shadow moved forward into its glow. Mina caught her breath and kept her hand on her small gun.

"Good evening, Miss Kolek. I returned to town yesterday and wanted to call on you this evening." The man removed his stylish hat; his chilly blue eyes reflected the flickering lamp light.

Mina's mouth grew dry. "It's rather late for a social call, Mr. Mathias."

Frank laid a hand on hers, and she tucked the pistol into his palm. He slid it into his coat sleeve. "Yes, it is, sir. I suggest you postpone your visit until her uncle approves."

The gambler's gaze skimmed over the young actor before returning to her.

"Perhaps, but I think this is the best time. You see, I've discovered a few things. It seems Dr. Cummings is not your betrothed; in fact, he's your cousin. I believe he left town today. How unkind of you to let me think otherwise. Besides, I hear, Mr. Johnson is also absent. I might overlook these slights. You see, my associates in St. Louis and Chicago think Denver holds promise for lucrative gambling establishments. I plan for all the growth and profit. In such, I need to find a wife."

Mina shuddered. "I don't know how I can assist you. We do not associate with the same people."

The man's lips twisted in a sneer. "That will change." Mr. Mathias stared at the pale light behind the upstairs window. His gaze returned to Frank. "Perhaps, I will wait until tomorrow."

Frank jumped down and came around to her side with a nonchalant stroll. However, Mr. Mathias reached her first. He reached up his well-groomed hand.

"Allow me, Miss Kolek."

Mina shivered and placed a tentative hand in his and jumped down and away before he offered more assistance.

Mr. Mathias tipped his hat. "I'll bid you a good evening and will return for a proper call soon."

Mina shivered again as the gambler disappeared into the darkness.

Frank looped the horse's reins around the post and moved to join her. She held out her hand. As Frank reached into his sleeve to retrieve her weapon, a man jumped from a passing wagon. He rushed at them. Frank tried to pull out the Derringer. The man drew back his arm and punched Frank hard. The gun dropped as Frank fell to the ground unconscious.

Mina dove for her weapon and screamed, but before she could reach it, the unknown assailant grabbed her, placing a hand over her mouth. A group of cowboys whooped as they rode down the street. Their drunken laughter dashed her hopes for a rescue. Her eyes darted to her fallen friend as the man pulled her to the now stopped wagon. Tears trickled down her cheeks. No possible horrors awaiting her dampened her desire to help Frank. She waited until the man's hand slipped while putting her into the wagon and then screamed at the top of her lungs.

"Uncle Silas!"

A hand struck Mina. Pain radiated along her cheekbone. Shock gripped her, shivers rippled through her body. "That was foolish, Miss Kolek." The man hit her again. Darkness reached for her. A distant voice said, "Take her to Holladay Street."

Chapter Eleven

Jack sighed upon packing his last belongings in his hotel room in Longmont. Since his September arrival in Fort Collins, he'd relished the fruition of his survey work—started months earlier—to bring the railroad tracks to the growing town, as well as the work around Longmont. The lines first built on paper from Wyoming, now stood actualized in steel rails on the ground. This brought Jack immense satisfaction. Both the Colorado Central Railroad and others at the expanding Union Pacific, as well as the Kansas Pacific assured him of continued work over the next few years. The problem stemmed from his continued indecision about Arkansas. Still, impending winter approached and unmet promises remained.

He glanced around his clean, nondescript room to be sure none of his belongings remained. Once satisfied, he checked the time before placing his watch in the lower right-hand pocket of his vest. The state-to-state and railroad line to railroad line time-variations, necessitated numerous resets of his timepiece during his travels. It felt good to be somewhat consistent for a while. The men who pushed to set consistent time zones had the right idea, just not the ability to get the necessary people to agree to this point. A smile tugged at his mouth. Sometimes he longed for the days of his childhood before the war. His father determined time by the passage and responsible use of daylight alone. He slid on his suit coat followed by his overcoat, the weight warmed and calmed him as he retrieved his hat and case and left the room.

A sharp whistle drew his gaze to a midsized man who stood in the lobby below as he started down the stairs. The smiling man's black suit matched his dark hair. Jack frowned when no flicker of recognition came. He shook the man's outstretched hand once he reached the bottom of the stairs.

"Bevil Henry," the man said.

Jack smiled. "No, sir. That is not my name. You must have mistaken me for someone else."

The man grinned, his hazel eyes sparkled. "That's possible, but I don't think so. No, let me try again. *I* am Bevil Henry, and your last name must be Johnson and your first is either Will or Jack. You look too much like your older brother, Marcus, to not be one or the other."

Jack set down his bag and placed his hat on top of it. He rubbed a hand across his face.

"You still have me at a disadvantage, sir. I am *Jack* Johnson, and Marcus is indeed my brother, but how do you know him?"

"I fought beside him for a bit before the Yanks took him prisoner at Gettysburg. I met him when his Third Arkansas regiment joined with our Texas Brigade. I also know John Wilkins and a few others you knew well. But the two I knew best were Richard Cushman and Matt Wilkins."

The last name brought a lump of suppressed emotion to Jack's throat.

"You knew Matt?"

The hazel eyes grew moist and the distinctive Texas accented voice choked a bit. "Yep. He became my best pard. I had a couple of years on him. He was fifteen, just shy of sixteen when we lost him at Chickamauga. I tried— anyway; I knew you must be Marc's brother."

Jack fought down his emotions. He'd grown up with Matt and still missed him. Memories distracted him until the man's expectant gaze refocused him. "That I am. It's unfortunate I didn't meet you sooner. I'm heading to Denver today."

The man shook his head and smiled again. He held up a basket. Delicious aromas wafted in the air. "So am I. I stopped by here to pick up some food from the café for the journey."

Jack grinned. "I ate a large breakfast to prevent the necessity. What line of work brings you to Colorado, Mr. Henry?"

"Please call me Bevil." The man spoke heavenward. "Matt, quit your laughing." He glanced back at Jack. "I'm an itinerant preacher. It's all because of Matt Wilkins—well not entirely—but the Good Lord used his life and death to change my direction. He saved my physical life in a roundabout way that day, as well as Richard's. I'll be happy to tell you about it during our journey today."

"Jack!"

A man rushed in the door.

"Daniel, why are you here?" Every muscle tensed at

the apparent distress on Daniel's face. "What's wrong? Is it Silas?"

Daniel stepped back to escort in a young woman who hovered at the door. He removed his hat and drew her forward.

"I went to Fort Collins to pick up Miss Shannon O'Connor, my new nurse, and planned to leave tomorrow, but I received a visit from a deputy yesterday, as well as a telegram from my uncle. I checked for you and found you'd come here yesterday. So we quickly made arrangements to arrive here this morning." Daniel glanced at Mr. Henry. "Who is this?"

Jack made rapid introductions.

"Jack, I feel so foolish," Daniel said. His desperate eyes moved from Jack to Bevil. "But there has not been any trouble for us since we returned to Denver. Uncle Silas is well now, and they are living with me over my office."

Jack's patience ended. "Daniel! Please tell me what's happened."

Daniel slumped and fingered the brim of his hat. He straightened and met his gaze. "Mr. Mathias has taken Mina. Well, we think he is to blame."

Jack clenched his jaw and waited for the young doctor to continue.

"One of the deputies arrived from Denver on other business yesterday and came to my hotel room. Uncle Silas asked him to find both of us. The deputy said Mina attended the Kellogg and Cary concert on Monday night. Her old friend, Frank, brought her home. Mathias awaited them there, outside of my office. Frank told him he needed to wait to call on Mina another time. He left. Then someone darted from the street, knocked out Frank, and took Mina. She managed to scream for our uncle, but they disappeared before Silas made it down the stairs. Neither the current lawmen, nor the shadowy vestige of a vigilante committee can confirm who took her. They talked to Mathias, but he claims he went home after his conversation with Frank and Mina. He says he did not even hear her scream."

Jack compressed his lips. He felt responsible. The reports his friend sent from Denver indicated no sign of the man since their return. Therefore, he had relaxed. After the level of infuriating spunk Mina displayed, he did not think any man capable of overcoming her. If only her physical stature matched her huge stubborn spirit.

"Let's go."

"Whoa, Jack." Bevil placed a hand on his shoulder. "You and Dr. Cummings look too much the gentlemen dandies to handle this. No offense. Don't you think the authorities should take care of it?"

"Bevil, don't let my clothes fool you. Underneath, I'm still cut from the same Arkansas fabric as my brother."

The man looked down at his own suit and grinned. "Well said. I hope we can resolve this without a fight, but on occasion in these parts, a fist of righteousness is well applied."

~

The reddish-blonde locks and cornflower blue eyes of Miss O'Connor drew appreciative looks from every man on the train. Eddie Rigby had mentioned her as a nursing friend of Hallie's in one of his letters to Jack. She'd helped Eddie and his mother surprise Hallie with a picnic during a visit to Boston at the end of her nursing school studies. If he remembered right, Eddie proposed to Hallie the day of that picnic. Jack well recalled his feelings of disappointment when Eddie declined to join him on a railroad job because of it.

Miss O'Connor appeared closer to his age than Hallie's. Of course, Hallie Hawkins Rigby started her nursing career later than others did.

"Miss O'Connor, did you graduate from nursing school at the same times as Hallie?" he asked.

She blushed once all eyes turned on her. "Later the next year. You see, Hallie started classes, but had to leave to attend to things in Georgetown—the one near Washington D.C.—for a bit. I didn't meet her until she returned to finish her courses in the autumn of '74. Her knowledge and caring heart really encouraged me. I am so delighted for her and Mr. Rigby. How long have you known them?"

"I only met them a short time before you did. You see, my older brother's best friend visited the family of Hallie's late husband that summer, and I went by to see him while in Washington on business. I left there with more friends than expected. It's still the best trip I've made."

She gave him a warm smile. "I understand. They are special."

A frown creased Dr. Cummings brow and Bevil Henry's elbow nudged Jack in the ribs. Jack grinned. Having a pretty hen share a smile in the midst of a coop of roosters stirred the dash of mischief layered underneath his well-tailored façade.

"I do hope they've not harmed Mina." Daniel's words served as a splash of cold water on those vying for Miss O'Connor's favor.

Jack felt guilty for his comparisons of the two women. Still, Shannon O'Connor made him smile. He liked it. Mina always made him want to scream. However, her trip across the country to find him made her deserving of his assistance. Maybe her captors might find her as irksome as he did and just let her go. He grinned before guilt sobered him. She'd be fine. She had to be. He remembered the first time he saw her in the wagon with Daniel in front of his mother's house. Her petite form and sparkling blue eyes had distracted him before Will required his full attention. He soon learned she merited more than a casual glance. No one should underestimate her.

He glanced at Daniel. "We can't do anything until we get there. Being in foul moods all the way to Denver won't help any of us."

Bevil cleared his throat. He stood. "Mr. Johnson, I think it's time for me to share a few war memories about your friends and brother. I'd prefer it to be in private. There are unoccupied seats near the back of the car. Let's go."

Jack took a deep breath and followed, he'd allow Bevil to distract all of them for a time. He traded apprehension about Mina's disappearance for the dread of revisiting the loss of one of his childhood friends. The same trepidation churned his insides before visiting the site of Marc's war imprisonment stirred anew. The loss of one of the youngest soldiers from his community stayed fresh under the scab of time. Picking at it did not seem wise to him, yet at the same time, a necessity. When Richard came home and shared about Matt's death, their families started healing, but for Will and him, Matt remained frozen in time. Matt marched away to war at thirteen, while, they—only a few years younger—stayed home. Not many of the original soldiers from Rockport returned after the war. Will used to say God spared them from soldiering by a breath. In many ways, Jack's desire to travel and take chances stemmed from the loss of Matt and the other soldiers. He grieved every time he turned a corner, eager to tell a story to a friend who no longer lived. It suffocated him even more once Marc finally came home, only to leave again. Going to school in Missouri helped, but he found those same feelings plagued him as he slept in his late cousin's room at his uncle's house. Will and Alice's marriage allowed him the freedom to travel to places where he didn't expect anything familiar, even as it now took away the welcome of home.

The smell of cigar smoke from across the aisle combined with his emotions brought bile to his throat once they found their new seats.

Bevil Henry's eyes held steady in somber reflection for a few moments. The black-haired man turned his head toward the window. As the scenery rolled forward, the reflection of the preacher's eyes mirrored the emotion of memories rolling backwards. A youthful grin formed on the now mature face. Bevil stroked his chin.

"We Texas boys strutted with bravado when we first met the men from the Third Arkansas Infantry. But we soon grew to respect their sharp shooting skills, their light-hearted ability to pillage for food from area farms with charm, and to respect those wicked knives many carried."

Jack cocked an eyebrow and reached down to slide

up his trouser leg to reveal the hilt of the knife stuck in his boot.

His companion chuckled. "That's the one. Anyway, being a little bit older than Matt, but still younger than many, I got to know him quick. Now, understand, the preacher you see before you, ain't the same wet-eared whelp. I was a simple Texas farm boy. Most of us came from many shades of poor, along with a few well-educated men as officers in the midst. War changed us all. You really come to know a man when you lie in the mud, bleed in the dirt, eat raw bacon, and even pick worms out of hard biscuits dunked in coffee together. I'm still amazed how Matt managed to keep his wide-eyed wonder and stoic thoughtfulness until the capture of Marc, John, and Boyd at Gettysburg. Without them to look out for him, he grew up fast. Richard tried, but as you lose men and have limited reinforcements to replace those losses— well, every man and boy must stand strong and battle smart. Matt became a tough soldier. I tried to get him to write to his Florey, but he thought she'd recognize the difference. He wanted her to wait for him, and determined she'd adjust to the changes in him better in person.

Anyway, those days at Chickamauga—such a blood-soaked mess—we got orders to take Viniard's Field—" Bevil's eyes misted and he tilted his head back, staring at the ceiling of the train car. "I sensed Matt's absence fighting at my side even before he called out to me. Blood spurted from his gut wound. I told him he was not dying in that field's trench grave. I lay on my belly and made him roll onto my back. Crawling and clawing my way out to slither the opposite way of the battle and back into the cover of trees almost defeated me, but we made it. The next impossibility came when we found Richard about to step out of the trees and onto the field with the next line of troops. He stayed with us and helped me get Matt to a field surgeon. We later found out most in his line died that day. I couldn't stop shaking when Richard carried Matt to the Doc. I slid down a tree trunk to sit on the ground. His blood ran off my back and made a puddle behind and underneath me. I'd always dismissed Matt's deep faith amidst all the hell around us. But *there*, I realized God's hand saved Richard, Matt, and hopefully me. Even after Richard came back to tell me Matt didn't make it, I remembered Matt saying he'd be fine even if he died. I came to know the Lord that day, Jack. All because of Matt's death. I've never been the same."

Tears coursed down Jack's cheeks, but when he raised his head, he found everyone around them involved in their own conversations. He wiped his face dry with the back of one hand and leaned forward.

"Bevil—" He stopped and straightened, staring at his knees. Silence hung between them until Bevil spoke.

"What happened to Florey?"

"What?" Jack glanced up to meet his new friend's eyes, wiping his nose with the back of his hand.

"What happened to Matt's Florey?"

Jack shook his head, took a deep breath, and gave a half-grin. "You won't believe it. Marc married her."

Bevil's mouth dropped open. "No."

Jack nodded. "Marc and John came close to death as prisoners of war at Ft. Delaware. Boyd took them to Texas—to his house—right after he secured their release. Boyd's wife and son both died of a bad fever before they arrived there. His brother had returned home a few days before them due to his war injuries."

Bevil shook his head. "Ben? I didn't even know he'd fought in the war. Boyd sure loved Nancy and couldn't wait to meet his son."

Jack nodded. "It devastated him. Anyway, they didn't make it back to Arkansas until the autumn of 1866. That's when Marc took notice of Florey."

"Hmmm." Bevil pinched his lip a couple of times and grinned. "Life is funny. Marc used to say only Matt could deal with such a strong headed girl. I think the Good Lord has a sense of humor."

The irony washed over Jack. Few things had turned out like any of them thought, but still—"I think so, too." He grinned. "They moved to Texas for a bit, but are now back in Arkansas. My pa got sick." Grief gripped him again. Silence ensued for a few moments.

"Are you a believer, Jack?"

Jack's head shot up, and he frowned. His insides churned with surprise and guilt. "Yes, I am. It happened my twelfth year. It's a struggle at times. I know I've made selfish choices."

"Stop, Jack," Bevil said. "Pray about it. Let it go and realize you've only traveled your road. You see, if you believe the Good Book, it tells us he uses everything for the best for his children. Even when things seem bad, it remains true. Look at Joseph and his brothers in the Old Testament."

Jack swallowed. His racing heart slowed. "Thank you."

The preacher smiled. Jack wondered about his brother's old friend.

"Bevil, are you, or were you married?"

"No."

Red crept into Jack's cheeks. Bevil laughed.

"Jack, I'm not a priest. I *can* marry. I haven't, and not because I haven't thought about it. You see, during the war, plenty of young ladies in the towns wanted to romance a soldier. I tasted those forbidden fruits early. Back then, nothing restrained me. Matt never strayed because of his faith and his feelings for Florey. Even Marc, John, and Boyd refrained. Many others did not feel the same need to deny themselves. But since the war, I've focused on the ministry He's given me. My pa and brother don't understand, but my ma is proud. We'll see. Why do you ask?"

Disappointment flooded Jack. "No, you won't do either if you've had experience with other ladies. I've got to see Miss Kolek settled and safe. We've got to find her and something like this can't ever happen again. I owe her uncle a great debt."

"I'm afraid I'm not following you, Jack." Bevil scratched the back of his head. "Why would—?"

"Miss Kolek is particular." Jack leaned forward, his elbows propped on his knees. "See, she came to Arkansas to find me with grand notions in her head. I've failed to satisfy any of them. She tried to find out about my experience with women. If you've had any, you do not measure up to her standards. I haven't and still am held in disfavor because I take an occasional drink."

"Do you know why?" Dr. Cumming's voice made them turn as he sat down beside Bevil, across from Jack.

Jack's mouth felt dry. Guilt stabbed at his gut. "Something about her friend?"

"Sally Morris, her best friend in college. A sweet young lady who fell in love with an experienced man. He loved her, mind you, but couldn't undo his past. He contracted a disease from his prior encounters and passed it to Sally after their marriage. When her health started to fail, she confronted him. He admitted his past to her but felt sure she'd be fine."

"That's what Mina said. If both of them returned to good health, why couldn't she forgive him?"

Daniel's eyes flashed. Jack held his breath.

"I can see she omitted a few things, Jack. By the time Sally sought medical help, her doctor said she'd never have children. Her health never returned. Contrary to what Mina told you, Sally died right before graduation. The loss devastated my romantic-hearted cousin. The hours of girlish talk about romance and marriage she'd shared with Sally—all now futile for her friend. Such circumstances only happened to the poor prostitutes in the mining camps and such. Right?" Daniel ran a finger across the bridge of his nose before he leaned forward, encompassing Jack and Bevil with the intensity of his regard as he continued. "The fact that such indiscretions could affect someone like Sally went against Mina's sense of justice and understanding. This is a real issue in our country. One of the leading doctors in Denver has advocated for health checks and licensing for the prostitutes there. It is a fight." Daniel near shouted the last words. He ducked his head as the porter hurried toward them.

"Is there anything amiss, Mr. Johnson?"

Daniel scooted back in his seat.

Jack reassured him with a smile. "No, Mr. Henderson. We are just having a needed discussion.

Sorry for the disturbance."

"Thank you, sir. Let me know if you gentlemen need anything."

The man tipped his hat and scurried toward the front of the car. Once the man departed the car, Jack cleared his throat and met the measured gaze of the doctor.

Daniel closed his eyes and rubbed his brow for a moment. He opened his eyes and dropped his hand into his lap. "Anyway, she talked to the preacher about it. He assured her God did not hold a causal role—facilitating her friend's suffering—in this, only sin. Still, the lack of rescue baffled her." He clenched his hand into a fist and shook his head. "Mina thought Sally's love for the man died. It didn't. Sure, Mrs. Morris was angry and hurt, but she really loved her husband. She forgave him before she died, but Mina could never accept it. The fact that Mr. Morris could still live a full life, while her friend died, still has her twisted inside. I tried to tell her the good it has wrought even last week."

When Jack started to speak, Bevil held up his hand. "Wait, Jack, I want to hear this before we offer any opinions."

Daniel's gaze moved to Bevil. "Thank you, Preacher. Anyway, Mr. Morris is a man of influence, and he has used his status to help some of the physicians trying to pass the legislation needed for licensing and health issues."

Jack released his breath on a slow current. Mina had a lot of pain and grief inside. He well understood the impact of those emotions, but not the way she applied it to others. "No, she didn't tell me the whole story. I don't know what to say, except to express my sorrow for the loss of her dear friend and those circumstances. Still, why does Mina take it on like it's her fight or her fate?"

"You see, Jack, there's more for you to consider before you judge my cousin. Mina takes things to heart. She only has limited memories of her parents during her first five years. Uncle Silas raised her more like a boy. She can shoot, hunt, skin game, cut wood, and all the things mountain life entails. You wouldn't know it in meeting the small, refined college woman. I grew up hearing about her parents, and knew about her living with Uncle Silas. When she came to live with us during college, she didn't let any of us see more than she wanted us to at first. But as time went by, she blossomed. Her intelligence and style enchanted us. I couldn't imagine her any other way. My own skepticism about her rough frontier past remained firm until we arrived in Denver. They took me to the old mountain cabin for three days, and got to see the survival side of her. You really don't know my cousin, Jack, so please don't try to procure a husband for her. Let's just find her and assure her well-being." He turned to Bevil. "No offense, Preacher."

Bevil shook his head. "None taken. But she sounds like someone I'd like to meet, if only to have the privilege of making her acquaintance."

Jack extended his hand toward Daniel. "I apologize."

Daniel shook his extended hand. "Indeed. However, I will admit she is outspoken. She also stands with those suffrage supporters."

"I'm sorry to hear that." Bevil Henry exhaled an

audible stream of air. "Women don't realize all the implications."

Jack scratched the back of his head. "She hunts?"

Daniel nodded.

"She sounds a bit like Florey." Jack smiled at Bevil. "Only, Florence won't hunt, but she can chop wood."

"Excuse me, but who is Florence?" Daniel asked.

"My sister-in-law, Marc's wife. You didn't meet her, but I'm beginning to think we should have let Miss Kolek meet more of my family." He slapped Bevil on the knee and laughed outright. "Then again, maybe not. Right, Bevil?"

Jack turned and met Daniel's dark eyes.

"Jack, I hope you realize how serious Mina's disappearance is."

Jack's throat constricted. He could only nod.

Bevil cleared his throat. He put his hand on Jack's shoulder.

"Dr. Cummings, I've only met Jack today, but I know his brother and knew many boys from his hometown. Most preferred a bit of fun, but when the battles came, those soldiers defined toughness. They became my brothers." His eyes held Jack's before glancing back to Daniel. "You can trust him."

Daniel stood. "I'm counting on it."

Jack watched him walk away and shook his head.

Bevil slapped him on the back. "Tell me about Boyd's family."

~

As soon as they arrived in Denver, they went to Daniel's office. He directed them up the stairs. Silas welcomed them while Daniel stayed downstairs to get updates on his patients from Dr. Brooks and put

Shannon O'Connor to work before he joined them.

"The mayor says no one's talking in the gamblers' district. Prostitutes, gamblers, and politicians who frequent those streets are silent about what happens there. In my opinion, even the city officials have a few tokens to spend in those brothels," Silas said.

Jack removed his coat. "Let's start at one end and visit every saloon and brothel. Someone knows *something*."

Bevil opened his pocket watch. "It's right before noon. Working in the daylight is safer."

Silas shook his head. "You're not well known in these parts. You'll get yourselves in trouble."

Jack smirked. "Maybe not well known, but I'm known by enough."

"Anyway, a friend of yours did stop by the morning after she went missing. He babbled his apologies for not watching her the night before and said he'd find her for us. I don't know why he thinks he can with all the other failed attempts," Silas said.

"So, that's what happened," Jack said. "That's Harry. He's an old friend I talked to after our encounter with Mr. Mathias on the train. His assignment included watching Mina every day until I returned. He owes me from an incident a few years ago, and I've also paid him for his efforts." His eyes met Bevil's. "We should start with him."

"Where?"

Jack's throat felt dry. Recollections of previous events close to the possible location indicated real danger for Mina. "Not far from where many of the gamblers stay."

The passage of time had only deepened the scrutiny

from Mr. Kolek. Jack squirmed under it.

"Jack Johnson, you sure have grown up since the day we met in the tunnel collapse. Daniel tells me you're a surveyor," Silas said.

His eyes met the wrinkle-framed brown ones. "Yes, sir, and I have you and my uncle to thank. You got me headed toward home, and I got as close as possible for me at the time. My uncle saw to my college. It seems something always keeps me from settling back in Rockport."

Silas stood silent for a few minutes.

"Jack, things are never as easy as 'seems' in life. Anyway, do you want me to come with you today?"

"Are you feeling well enough?"

"Yep."

Jack nodded. "Let's go."

~

Jack found Harry leaning against a post outside of a popular brothel. The red-haired Irishman flushed.

"Will you be accepting my apology, Jack? I had no idea Mathias returned to town. Nothing eventful before then. I allowed myself to go home when her friend escorted her toward *her* home in a buggy after the concert. Anyway," Harry said, puffing his chest under the red suspenders, "I've found her. It's taken some doing. Not even Miss Millie knows one of her girls has her there. Lily is involved with Mathias. It's plain she's not seemed respectable enough to marry—until now—I heard Mathias sent for a preacher. The strange thing is this; Mr. Mathias isn't parading about town as usual. No one has seen him much since his return to town."

"Tell us where," Jack said.

The man inclined his head as he rubbed the toe of

one shoe on the back of the opposite pants leg. "Upstairs here." He pushed away from the post "We need to go in the back way and be quick. He sent a boy out for a preacher about an hour ago."

Bevil cleared his throat. Jack nodded. The divine attention to details chilled and warmed him at the same time.

"After you direct us to the specific room, you come back and watch for the preacher. Stop him on his way because we already have a minister with us. That's how we get in there. Just say you've brought a preacher."

Bevil tapped his shoulder.

"He doesn't know you're in town, Jack. Let's not alert him—yet. Let me go inside and see how this unfolds. We aren't *sure* Mr. Mathias is involved."

Jack frowned. "The chances he's not are slim, but you're right. I'll keep out of sight for a bit."

Silas, Harry, and Jack went in the back, while Bevil entered through the front door. They crept up the stairs unseen. At the top, an empty hallway lay to the right. Shut doors along the wall, as well as the mumbles and unspeakable sounds emitted from the closed rooms assisted their undetected progress along the rug-covered path. A loud commotion with squeals, screams, and sounds of a fight in the next hall ahead reached them. The men exchanged looks and crept to a vantage point just around the corner from the site of the fray. Jack waved Silas and Harry back behind him before peeking.

A man lay not more than a foot away from them, bloodied and unconscious in the hallway in front of an open door. Mr. Mathias's voice reached them from inside the room.

"My dear Miss Kolek, I'm so glad my unexpected

visit to Miss Lily today has allowed me to rescue you." The gambler's voice switched from soothing to angry. "Lily, how could you work with such a man? How many ladies have you snatched?"

"George, I only do what's needed to survive." The woman's voice held no vestige of apology. "I profit from finding ladies to marry certain men who've settled in the areas around Denver."

"But why choose Miss Kolek?"

"Well—you mentioned her a few times. Let's just say, I wanted to see her well matched."

Jack and the others heard a muffled protest.

"Lily, remove the cloth from her mouth."

Chair legs wobbled and scooted on the wooden floorboards, followed by female sputters and protests.

Mina's voice cracked. "How dare you? You better let me go at once. I'll see to my own reputation."

"I agree, Miss Kolek. I'm appalled," Mr. Mathias said.

"So you *say*."

Jack grinned at Mina's skeptical reply.

"Here, let me untie you." The creak of wood reached the eavesdropping trio. "I came here to marry Miss Lily today; ironic given the circumstances."

An audible female gasp preceded the gambler's next words.

"However, I now see my hopes for her are not worth my endeavors. Please know I had no idea of her actions, Miss Kolek. I do hope this doesn't impact your cousin's practice or your uncle."

"What do you mean?" Mina asked in a hoarse voice.

"You may think you can preserve your good name

as I've rescued you, but people still may talk. How many days since they took you?"

"Since the night of the concert."

"Hmmm—we can hope it will be fine, or—"

"Or *what*, Mr. Mathias?"

Harry held his finger to his lips as Bevil strode past them and into the room.

"The young man directed me to this room for a wedding." A brief period of silence ensued. "What's happening here? I'll send for the authorities!"

"No, no, sir. This is a misunderstanding. I am George Mathias. I have remedied this unfortunate situation. There is no need to cause Miss Kolek public embarrassment."

Bevil's voice held grudging consideration. "I still think this young woman and the man in the hall need medical attention."

"I'll see to it, sir. But I do want to complete my business here first," Mr. Mathias said.

Bevil's response ignored Mr. Mathias. "Ma'am? I don't think her care needs to wait."

"Well, Mr. Mathias did rescue me." Mina's voice quivered and broke. "He doesn't need to assist me further. I can wait a few minutes if *you* will take me to my cousin?"

"Of course. Who is your cousin, ma'am?"

"Dr. Daniel Cummings."

"Oh, you are the one everyone is searching for! You're Mina Kolek?" Footsteps sounded inside the room. "No, don't try to stand. Here let me help you, Miss Kolek. Sit back down." Irritation crept into Bevil's next words. "Then let's be about your business, Mr. Mathias. The young man fetched me here to perform a wedding. Is there to be a wedding? Which one of these women is the bride?"

"This is my man, and I am the bride," Lily said.

A long pause followed before Mathias commented.

"No, not anymore, Lily. Miss Kolek, I'd be happy to marry *you* and protect your good name."

Jack placed a finger to his lips. He wanted to take Mr. Mathias by complete surprise. They crept to the opposite wall outside the doorway and managed to avoid the still unconscious man on the hallway floor. Silas moved from the wall into the room. Jack and Harry followed him.

Mina's hair hung around her shoulders in disarray. Her clothes hung in torn, rumpled folds. Tears streamed down her pale face and dripped off her bruised jaw.

"Uncle Silas." Mina swayed on the chair. Her uncle rushed to catch her in his arms.

Jack's eyes hardened when Mathias looked his way.

The gambler crossed to Silas. "I am glad you've found her, Mr. Kolek. I only wish my assistance had come sooner. If I'd stayed to visit with her longer the other night, I might have prevented this."

The skeptical look Silas sent Mr. Mathias over his niece's head conveyed his opinion.

"We will sort out the exact circumstances of these events with the police chief and the sheriff once I get my niece home."

"No, Uncle Silas." Mina pulled back. "I can't let you do that. Mr. Mathias is right. This might mean trouble for you and Daniel's new practice. People love to gossip."

"But, Mina, the sheriff is aware of your absence. They rode out again this morning."

She licked her parched lips. Tears spilled down her face. "Once he returns, tell him I ran off to get married and have returned."

Silas placed his hands on both of Mina's arms and steadied her to meet his eyes.

"You are not marrying Mr. Mathias. I'll not allow it."

"Mr. Kolek, let me assure you. I'll see—"

Jack refused to listen to any more of this. He stepped forward.

"You'll leave her alone, Mr. Mathias. We appreciate your assistance—circumspect though it is."

The gambler's icy blue eyes met his. "I think we should consider Miss Kolek's wishes. She *is* of age."

Jack looked at Mina. She lifted her chin.

"He is correct, Mr. Johnson. Uncle Silas, I want to protect our name."

Silas squatted in front of her and, once on eye level, held her chin steady. "Mina, did that other man—?"

She blushed and a tear trickled down her cheek. Her hand shook as she reached for her uncle's. "No, he inspected me a bit— I am—who'd have me?"

"Maybe your friend Frank?"

"So he's all right?" she asked.

"Yes, he's still bruised but fine."

Mina's tears fell faster, and her shoulders shook.

Silas tried to gather her to him, but she pushed away.

"No, no, Uncle. I need to decide this. Your suggestion is not fair to Frank. He is more like a brother. There is no one else."

Jack's mouth went dry. He kept his voice soft. His heart beat faster. "There's me, Miss Kolek."

Her soft, tear-filled blue eyes lifted to him and widened. "You?" She blinked a couple of times, used the back of her hand to swipe away the moisture on her cheeks, and straightened her back. "I think not, Mr. Johnson."

Irritation rose inside Jack but subsided when devastation and confusion replaced the momentary assertiveness on Mina's face. He reached in his pocket for his handkerchief and stepped forward. An awkward pause hung between them before determination filled him. He dabbed at her eyes. She took the white cloth from him. The moment tingled and then stung.

"No . . . no . . . please . . .," she choked out before she broke into uncontrollable sobs.

Silas cleared his throat. "Mina, you may refuse Mr. Johnson, but I say the same regarding Mr. Mathias. So it's settled. There will be no marriage. We are going home now."

A low boil of emotion quaked inside Jack. His eyes lingered on Mina for a brief moment before he spun on his heel and stepped over the still unconscious man. Harry hovered in the hall. Jack whispered instructions to him before he strode away and down the back stairs.

The sour smells of sewage and whiskey filled his nostrils as he passed through the back door. He mounted his horse and waited.

Bevil emerged with Mina and Silas. She held his handkerchief to her nose.

Silas swung into his saddle and reached down as Bevil assisted Mina up in front of him. Silas turned up the collar on Mina's coat and reached for the reins. While Jack waited for Bevil to mount his horse, he glanced at his pocket watch, grateful for the hour of the day. A few people stared as they passed down the street, but none bothered them.

Daniel met them in front of his office and ushered Mina inside. Jack and Bevil returned their rented horses to the livery stable.

~

Mina turned her head and screamed into the pillow. Daniel tried to calm her to no avail. The thought of an examination by any man, even her cousin, at this point, deepened her distress. She pushed his hands away.

"Mina, calm down. It's only me. We need to examine you," Daniel said.

Her eyes pleaded with Miss O'Connor over her cousin's shoulder.

"Excuse me, Doctor, but maybe I could talk to her and do a cursory examination for now," Miss O'Connor said.

Mina's heart pounded. Daniel raised his eyebrow and she nodded.

"Very well. I'll check on our other patients. Call out if you need me, Miss O'Connor."

"Yes, Dr. Cummings."

Miss O'Connor took Mina's cold hands.

Mina shut her eyes. The mention of the other patients in the waiting room mortified her. They'd seen her. She opened her eyes. Miss O'Connor squeezed her hand.

"How can I ever face our neighbors and friends? What they must think of me," Mina said.

"They aren't. Most of the ones out there are preoccupied with their own maladies. A mild interest and concern for you is the most I'd anticipate. How much did you notice about them? Who did you see?"

Mina thought for a moment. She couldn't recall the identity of one person they'd ushered her past. Shannon's words humbled her. She started to laugh, soft at first, but she lost control and vacillated between hysterical laughter and tears. Shannon gathered her into her arms on the edge of the examination cot.

"I don't understand any of this, Shannon. Where's Uncle Silas?"

"Your uncle will be back this evening. He wanted Dr. Cummings to tend to you first. Are you up to telling me a bit of it, Mina? It will help direct me in your examination. After that, we can get you upstairs to your own bed."

Mina's last strand of self-reliance unfurled. The story tumbled out amid this new plague of uncharacteristic tears mixed with moments of familiar control. Shannon eased her back onto the pillow and covered her with a blanket as she finished.

Shannon cleaned her scratches and scraps prior to a discreet examination and a cloth and basin bath. The aroma of soap comforted Mina. Shannon smoothed Mina's hair away from her face.

"I'll brush your hair once I get you into a gown upstairs, Mina. Let me go get, Dr. Cummings," Shannon said.

She'd let Shannon share as needed with Daniel. The one thing she wouldn't share with Shannon, and didn't want to admit to herself, bothered and bolstered her the most. Even though she'd prayed *he'd* rescue her, she'd treated Jack with open and public disdain. Why?

~

For once in his life, Jack found he didn't want to

talk. He appreciated Bevil's compatible silence during the walk back to Dr. Cumming's office.

Nurse O'Connor met them at the door.

"Since Mina is with us, Mr. Kolek went to the store to finish work needed by Mrs. Cosgrove. He asked you to meet him for dinner at the hotel closest to the train station."

"Thank you, Miss O'Connor," Jack said.

"You're welcome, Mr. Johnson. If you want to see Dr. Cummings, he should be back from upstairs in a little while."

"How is she?" Jack asked.

"I tucked her into bed a few minutes ago and she's resting. The doctor went to check on her after I relieved him of the patients here."

Jack took in the handful of people in the office. A boy held his arm and moaned. Jack grinned, thinking about when he broke his own arm jumping out of the tree by the barn at about the same age. An older man with a cough and two cowboys, one with either a gunshot or knife wound to the thigh, sat by the window.

"We'll use the outside stairs."

"Very well," Miss O'Connor said.

Harry paced outside the office; oblivious to the pedestrians he bumped in the process. He tipped back his derby style hat as they approached.

"Jack, you were right."

Jack choked back a curse. He glanced at the wagons and horses on the busy street in front of them.

"Let's go upstairs to hear about it."

Daniel opened the door. "I heard you coming. Come in, but we need to be as quiet as possible. Mina is finally sleeping."

They left their coats and hats on the hooks by the door and moved to the table. Each tried to make as little noise as possible. Once seated, Jack nodded to Harry. The red-haired young man leaned forward and began.

"You might not like the telling of it, but Jack's feelings about Mathias are well justified. After you left, I ducked into the next room. Found it empty, but—" His cheeks reddened. "As I previously passed an evening there, I know how thin the walls are. Miss Lily started laughing. She asked how she did, and Mathias chuckled and said she did well. No one would suspect that he'd arranged everything. He wants Mina to feel beholden to him and wants to marry her to have a better position in Denver, while still keeping Miss Lily."

Daniel hunched over the table. Anger burned in his eyes when he lifted his head. "This is beyond reason. Do you know what he subjected her to? Mina finally broke down and told Miss O'Connor. From what she could gather amid my cousin's uncharacteristic hysteria, in addition to the kidnapping, he let a strange man lay his hands on her, short of ruining her. That woman kept her in her room behind a thin dressing screen—tied and gagged— while she entertained her customers. Jack—"

"Can do nothing, Daniel," Bevil said. "Your cousin refused Jack's honorable offer of marriage. I hate to say it, but your cousin might need to return to Illinois and start again. It doesn't appear Mr. Mathias plans to leave at this time. We can tell the chief of police and the sheriff, but there's no guarantee of anything."

Jack rubbed his hands over his face. He released his breath but not the frustration within. He noticed her hat and coat on the hook by the door. The haunting memory of her devastated face lingered.

"Might I check on her, Daniel?"

Daniel lifted his eyebrows. He widened his stance and crossed his arms, looking more like a protective brother rather than a cousin. "Why?" he said

Jack frowned, wracking his brain for a sensible answer. No feasible response came for his three friends, but something inexplicable churned within his gut. He shook his head.

"I just need to, Daniel."

Mina's cousin hesitated but nodded. Daniel touched Jack's shoulder as he walked past him. "Don't wake her," Daniel said.

~

Soft breaths emanated from the bed in the otherwise silent room. Jack suspended all inhalations while shutting the door behind him, holding the knob to control its slow rotation before it latched. The rustle of the sheets under the quilt-topped mound of covers drew his gaze. The dim light from the curtained window revealed Mina's face. He waited for her eyes to flutter open, but her post-trauma repose held her fast. Her small, delicate features resembled a cameo in silhouette. He leaned his head back against the door and gave a slow release to the air in his lungs.

The only other woman he'd watch sleep was his mother during an illness, but this felt different. Mina's dark eyelashes, her red cupid's-bow lips, and velvet complexion—marred only by the bruise on her jaw—mesmerized him. The cascade of dark hair, with tendrils splayed around her gown-covered arms and shoulders transfixed him.

The darkness concealed the sprinkle of freckles on

her nose. Jack smiled. His mind went back to their first meeting. Her beauty had washed over him then, as it did now.

Of course, the quiet of sleep prevented her often scathing and judgmental looks and words toward him. He grinned and dropped his head. Who could blame her? Her experiences with him did not recommend him for much else. The desire to change that flamed inside of him. A gentle urging within his spirit guided him, sinking him to his knees. His soft words broke the silence–only audible to someone straining to listen and to his Creator.

"Dear Father, You know my failings and sins. Forgive me and guide me. Thank You for using Marc and Mina to prevent me from giving into temptations.

"It's not clear what You have planned, but I do know my being here with Silas Kolek's family is not chance, and neither was meeting him all those years ago.

"Therefore, I'm listening, Lord.

"But now, I pray for Mina. Thank You for guiding us to find her and bring her home. Please help her recover from this terrible experience.

"Lord, I can't help telling You—Mathias and his friends make me mad. You know that. When Harry told me Mathias is responsible for everything I—forgive me, again. Anyway, help Mina see him plain. She's special. The man You have for her will appreciate her quick mind and bold heart. She makes me think. Anyway, Lord, please take care of her.

"In Jesus's name—Amen."

Jack opened his eyes and stared at the floorboards for a moment. As he raised his head, his breath caught.

Mina's eyes met his, tears spilling over and down her cheeks.

His chest constricted. No sneaking out undetected, so he sighed and stood. The words to explain or defend himself rushed forward but ebbed away without utterance.

He crossed to her bedside and brushed the moisture away from her cheeks with a few gentle swipes of his finger. She cried harder. He longed to gather her in his arms and comfort her. Instead, he knelt down by her bed and took her hand. No words seemed adequate, so he just let her cry. Once her shoulders ceased to shake and her breathing regulated, he squeezed her hand and stood. She stared up at him with puffy eyes. He gave her a gentle smile.

"Mr. Johnson—"

He shook his head.

"It's *Jack*, Mina. You rest."

He closed the door with his heart pounding. It continued to pound when he reached the other room where her family and his friends still sat at the dining table.

"How is she?" Bevil asked.

Jack ran a hand through his hair. "Well, she—"

Successive knocks sounded at the door.

He motioned Daniel back to his seat as he continued to the door and opened it.

The concern in the blue eyes of the curly blonde-haired young woman turned to confusion.

"Who are you?"

Jack grinned at the small, but amply rounded female. She resembled the paintings of cherubs on display in city art galleries.

"I'm Jack Johnson. I gather you're here to see Miss Kolek."

She eyed him up and down, blinked, and blushed. "You're . . . You're Jack Johnson? Oh, my."

She gaped at him until Daniel joined them at the door.

Daniel placed one hand on his shoulder. Then Daniel took his other hand and made a sweeping, head to toe, presentation gesture of Jack. "Yes, Miss Singer, *this* is the no longer mysterious Jack Johnson." He straightened and said, "Jack, this is Mina's best friend, Betsy Singer. Come in, please"

The blue eyes continued to stare as she entered until she spotted the men at the table.

They stood and she scurried toward Bevil.

"Why, Pastor Henry, what are you doing here?"

Bevil's perplexed eyes met Jack's over the young woman's head before giving her an apologetic smile.

"I'm afraid you have me at a disadvantage, Miss Singer. Have we met?"

She laughed—a contagious, bubbling sound, causing them all to join in without knowing why.

"Yes, actually, we have—about five years ago, when I visited my relatives in our old mountain village. You preached there."

"Please forgive me, Miss Singer. Being a traveling preacher sometimes fills my head with more names than faces." Bevil inclined his head. "Is Isaac Singer your uncle?"

"He is," Betsy said.

"Well, it is nice to see you. I won't forget our meeting this time," Bevil said with a warm smile. "Anyway, I am an old friend of Mr. Johnson's brother.

We served in the war together."

"You must have been a very young soldier."

"Yes."

"Miss Singer, let me take you to Mina," Dr. Cummings said. "Unless she is still resting, I know she'll want to see you." He turned to Jack. "Is she still sleeping?"

Jack averted his eyes and mumbled, "She stirred before I left the room." He turned to look at the mantle clock. "Bevil, I need to meet Silas. Do you want to walk with me?"

"Yes, I do."

Jack noticed the empty chair beside Bevil. "Where's Harry?"

Bevil walked around the table and retrieved their hats and coats by the door. He handed Jack his.

"Harry went to inform the authorities about Mathias. He said to tell you to stop by to see the deputy first. We have some time before Silas expects you." Bevil turned, extending his hand. "Dr. Cummings and Miss Singer, I enjoyed meeting you."

"Likewise, Preacher," Daniel said. He shook Bevil's hand and turned to Jack. "I'm going back to the office since Miss Singer is here for Mina. Please tell Uncle Silas."

"I will."

Chapter Twelve

Jack descended the stairs two at a time and strode down the street.

"What dog's nipping at your heels, Jack? Slow down," Bevil muttered.

"Harry's right. I need to see a deputy. We need to pay Mr. Mathias another visit before we meet Silas," Jack said.

"From the look on your face, I'd better start praying for a few angels to be with us."

"I think that's an excellent idea. Are you sure you want to go with me, Bevil?"

"Yep."

Within the hour, Bevil and Jack entered the saloon where Mr. Mathias sat at the card table. He glanced up at their approach but didn't stop his play.

"Pull up a chair, gentlemen," Mr. Mathias said.

"I must decline, Mr. Mathias. However, I'd like to give you an update on Miss Kolek if you will excuse yourself," Jack said.

Mr. Mathias smiled at the others around the table.

He pushed back his chair and stood. "If you gentlemen will pardon me from taking your money for a time, I must take my leave." The gambler turned toward Jack. "Please follow me to my office. I assume my ownership of this establishment is not surprising to you."

Jack did know.

They followed him. Once inside the office, the gambler shut the door and started toward his desk. Jack nodded at Bevil, who moved to stand with his back against the door.

Jack drew his knife from his boot and pushed the man against the wall behind his desk. He placed the curved knife tip under the gambler's chin and stared into the cold depths of his eyes.

"We have a witness to your admission of arranging for the abduction of Miss Kolek. Furthermore, the man who actually nabbed her is now in the sheriff's custody. You will soon find yourself sharing a jail cell."

"I doubt that—"

Jack dug the tip of the knife into the skin under the sneering man's chin bone. A drip of blood coursed down the blade.

"Don't speak, Mathias. You will accompany me to the sheriff without a disruption. And, no matter the outcome, you will have no further contact with Miss Kolek. Do you understand? Blink if you do."

Mathias blinked. Jack eased the knife tip away but kept Mathias pinned against the wall.

"Why would you put her through that ordeal?" Jack demanded.

Jack's fingers twitched on his knife's hilt when Mathias smirked.

"Miss Kolek traveled across the country to meet a

man she'd never met. Yes, I learned the truth. It seems you've tried to keep it from me. You didn't meet her expectations. Therefore, I decided to be her hero. That's not a crime."

The back door swung open and both the sheriff and a deputy stood there.

"But arranging for abduction is, Mr. Mathias. The police and I agree. We'll take it from here, Mr. Johnson. It's a good thing our vigilante committee isn't still in charge," the sheriff said.

The glacier gaze of Mr. Mathias turned on Jack as they escorted him to the door.

"My attorney will contest this for me, but at least she refused you, Mr. Johnson. It seems we must both do without her charms."

The lawmen hustled Mathias through the doorway.

Bevil took the knife, wiped it with a handkerchief, and returned it. Jack slid it into his boot and pulled his pant leg over it.

"You're more like your brother than you know, Jack."

Those words compounded the satisfaction Jack felt.

"Then, at least I have some virtues."

"You Arkansas boys get the job done. What time are we meeting Mr. Kolek?"

Jack pulled out his pocket watch. A quick glance determined his answer. "In about ten minutes." He slid it back into his vest just as Harry appeared in the back doorway wearing a grin.

"Are we even, my friend?

"That we are, Harry. Thank you."

Harry glanced over his shoulder and rubbed his hands together. He tipped his hat and licked his lips.

"I'll be taking my leave of you. A mite of refreshment is in order. If you be taking my meaning?"

They laughed.

"Take care of yourself," Jack said.

"I'll be praying for you," Bevil said.

"You do that, Preacher," Harry said with a twinkle in his eyes. He whistled all the way out the door.

~

Jack and Bevil arrived at the restaurant as the gray winter sky seeped into evening darkness.

Silas gestured to the chairs opposite him. Jack noticed the strain etched in his friend's aged face. They pulled off their gloves and stuffed them into their coat pockets.

"Mr. Mathias and his accomplices are in custody," Jack said.

"Thank you, Jack."

"You're welcome. Also, I checked on Mina. She allowed me to hold her hand while she cried for a bit. Betsy's with her now. It'll take her some time."

Silas leaned back in his chair and rubbed the side of his nose with one finger. He narrowed his eyes and stared until Jack started to squirm in his chair before he spoke. "She allowed you to take her hand and cried in front of you?"

"Only a bit–I woke her. It may have been the sight of me," Jack said, shrugging.

"She did decline your offer of marriage," Bevil said.

"I can't blame her. You know– if I'd handled things with my brother Will like my pa told me to in his letter—"

"How's that?" Silas asked.

Jack drummed two fingers on the table for a moment.

"Well, Pa told me Will might brawl with me, and I shouldn't run from it—give him the fight he wanted but to let him win. Pa wanted me to know right or wrong doesn't matter where forgiveness is concerned, and Will needs me more than he allows. He wrote about my brother's hard work. I'm the only one who wouldn't come home, so Will thinks of himself as the king rooster. My pa wanted me to allow my brother that because, and I don't know why my father thought this, my heart allows me more than Will's pride lets him tolerate. I've re-read his letter so many times—" He hung his head and swallowed the lump in his throat. "I failed my pa's last wish. My anger and pride got in the way. Because of it, Mina got a very poor first impression."

Bevil cleared his throat, and he turned to look at him.

"Jack, we all fail and sibling disputes have led to worse than a lost fight. You still can seek your brother's forgiveness. Even if you feel he wronged you."

"I *did* write him a letter and mailed it before we left Fort Collins."

Bevil slapped his hands on the table. "Then it's done. I know God and your pa are well satisfied, whether Will accepts it or not. It's your brother's decision now."

"I agree, Jack," Silas said. "Are you going to try to return to Rockport again?"

Jack unbuttoned his coat as the temperature inside started to suffocate him a bit.

"I've been offered more surveying work here and

also received a telegram from Hot Springs. Both start in early spring. I have a little time off for the winter. Before the weather gets too bad, I have to decide. Should I head to Arkansas or stay here in Denver for the winter?"

Silas crossed his arms and nodded. His thoughtful stare made Jack squirm again. The old man's eyes cut to Bevil, until he also shifted in his chair. Silas chuckled—a deep sound, rough like creaking leather on a saddle.

"You two don't stay put very long."

"How did I get involved in this?" Bevil asked.

"Jack, I tried to guide *you* off that way of life the first time we met. Preacher, I can't speak to your reasons, but I think it has something to do with your war experience."

Jack extended his hand until Silas took it. They shook and released.

"I want to thank you for your advice back then. Unbelievably, I tried and got as close to home as possible at the time. I returned to my uncle's and finished college because of you."

Silas leaned forward. "You're welcome for the better job situation because of your schooling, but you're still not settled and no better than a vagabond."

A trace of defensiveness stirred. Jack leaned back in his chair. "I tried to go home."

"What *is* home, Jack? Bevil?" Silas stroked his beard. "I found mine wherever the wind took me until Mina came, and I had someone who needed me. That settled me after a time. She moved around with me at first. Now, I have a place here even if Mina marries and leaves. She taught me what matters."

"Mr. Kolek, my choice has been a spiritual one," Bevil said. "I became a Christian during the war, and the ministry became my way of life. For now, being itinerate is where God wants me. Although, I am free to marry and pastor a permanent church, that door hasn't opened to this point. I'll follow His guidance."

Silas smiled through his whiskers. "I'll concede to Him on that. You'll do, Preacher." His age-crinkled eyes cut to Jack.

"I tried here too, Silas. Your niece turned me down in your presence."

"I did hear her, Jack. That's not it. I'm talking about you getting still long enough to get your bearings. Stay with us through the winter. Get quiet. Go up to my old cabin. My friend Toby is up there. He's peaceable and has enough provisions for the winter. He's a great hunter."

Jack's stomach churned with hunger, as well as indecision. He still needed more time to think about everything in his heart. For now, he'd settle for a full plate. "Do you mind if we get dinner before chewing on this further? The smell of food around us is more than I can ignore."

"Come to think of it—we didn't eat much of anything today," Bevil said.

"That's allowed. Even my old stomach might tolerate a bite or two," Silas said, patting his stomach. "The food's not bad here, although Mina's cooking is better. No thanks to me. Mrs. Cosgrove taught her."

An hour later, dinner finished, they walked into the hotel lobby.

"I'll say good night. A local pastor and his wife expect me to stay with them," Bevil said.

Silas shook Bevil's hand.

"Jack, if you decide to stay with old Toby, get word to me, and I'll get you there. The folks in those parts expect me there this month," Bevil said.

"I'll do that. When are you leaving?"

"By Monday morning."

"That'll give you both a couple of more days," Silas said.

"I'll stop by and let you know either way, Silas. G'Night," he said.

Jack watched them exit, shivered at the blast of icy air coming through the door, and turned to make his way upstairs.

Chapter Thirteen

Whimpering and crying roused Mina. She frowned, but her eyes felt too heavy and swollen to open.

The familiar smell of her uncle's pipe tobacco preceded the sway of the mattress as the ropes underneath gave way to someone. Flashes of occasional childhood nightmares during storms emerged. Then, as now, Uncle Silas came to her. He touched her forehead with the back of his hand.

"Mina, wake up, little one. Make the dreams go away."

She turned her head from side to side a few times before forcing her swollen eyelids to lift. "Uncle Silas?"

"Yes, Mina. Your cries woke me."

"I'm sorry."

He stroked her hair. "None of that. You've endured too much this week, my dear."

She bit at her thumbnail for a moment. "It's not something I want to ever repeat. Please know the man did not spoil me. He touched, grabbed, and kissed me a few times but stopped for some reason. I don't care why." Heat flooded her cheeks at the memory. "Being tied to the chair and unable to fight bothered me the most. That and the sound of the activities in the next room, as well as in the room where they held me—I can't." She folded over the edge of the sheet peeking out from under the quilt and pulled it up to her neck. "Those women there are—different. I could never do what they do for money. Circumstances trap them. Anyway, I'm so grateful to Mr. Mathias."

"Mina—" Her uncle's warning tone held unwanted confirmation.

She squinted at him. "What? Oh, Uncle Silas, you don't believe what Mr. Johnson said? I mean, I heard him say something about Mr. Mathias being responsible for that man grabbing me. I've thought about it. It can't be true. I mean, I know Mr. Mathias is not someone I've ever trusted, but his actions in rescuing me yesterday proved him otherwise."

"Mina, he did it."

Mina pulled away as disbelief gave way to defensiveness. Why would Mr. Mathias rescue her if he did it? The thought of the gambler's feigned concern sparked her anger into a steady flame. "How?"

"Jack confronted him and the lawmen heard his admission."

Mina released the covers to give an angry swipe at her tears. She kicked her feet in frustration. "I wish to stop this infernal weeping. It's not like me."

The door opened and Daniel stood in the doorway. He yawned.

"I'd hoped you'd sleep through the night after Betsy helped you bathe this afternoon."

"Daniel, you sound more like a cousin than a doctor right now," Mina said.

Daniel propped against the doorframe. He rubbed his eyes. "I beg your pardon, Mina. I've only been home for an hour. Miss Simpson is very ill with pneumonia. She refuses the hospital and insists on treatment at home."

Daniel carried the lantern he held into the room. "Sit up, my dear cousin. I can hear how congested your nose is from crying. You must be thirsty from breathing through your mouth. Uncle Silas, we need to get her some water and extra blankets or pillows to elevate her."

Mina sat up and made a face at them. This must stop—they acted as if an illness plagued her. Distraught? Yes, more than a bit, but their coddling felt worse.

"No, no, no. I appreciate and love both of you, but you will be the ones sick if you don't get rest. What time is it, Daniel?"

"Around four in the morning."

Silas stood and started for the door. "I'll be back with some water."

Mina threw back the covers and swung her legs over the side of the bed. She stood and put her hands on her hips. "I don't want to sleep. Both of you need to do so. Sleep for at least another hour. I'll have breakfast ready."

Her uncle frowned. "Mina—"

"Uncle, please. I need normal inside these walls. Goodness knows what the whispers and gossip are about me in town."

Daniel shook his head as she pushed past him.

Mina stood by the door. She tapped her foot as they continued to stare at her in sleepy disbelief. "Please go to your rooms. I need to use the chamber chair and dress."

Those words hastened the men's exits. She shut the door.

An hour and a half later, the smell of bacon, biscuits, eggs, and coffee tantalized her family awake. Mina wiped her hands on her apron and smiled. A knock on the door startled but did not surprise her.

Once she smoothed the loose tendrils of hair away from her face, she opened it. Instead of the expected patient in need of Daniel, Jack Johnson and the preacher from her rescue stood outside the threshold.

"Good morning, gentlemen. Won't you come in? My uncle and cousin should join us soon. Please have a seat at the table. I've made a large breakfast."

Unexpected tears sprang to her eyes and she hurried to the stove.

Mina poured the coffee as her cousin and uncle joined them.

"Good morning," Daniel said.

Silas pulled out his chair. "What brings you out so early? Especially you, preacher?"

"Jack knocked on the door very early this morning," Bevil said.

Bevil did not elaborate. Jack smiled at him.

"Preachers and doctors don't seem to mind so much. I'm thankful his hosts didn't take offense. Anyway, Silas, I want to winter with your friend Toby," Jack said.

"Why?" Mina bit her lip and tapped her foot under her skirt. "Why would you stay with Toby?

Uncle Silas gave her a warning look, softened by a tolerant smile. "Because I offered, and he has the time before his next work situation starts. May I have coffee and breakfast now, Mina?"

"Yes, sir," Mina said.

Mina poured the coffee, placed the plates, and brought the platters. The men made her glad of her ample preparations, except for the limited amount on the preacher's plate. "Is something wrong with the bacon, Preacher Henry?"

"No, ma'am. Please don't be offended. We ate bacon good, bad, and raw during the war. My stomach prefers not to recall those memories."

"Oh, I'm so sorry. I can make you a few slices of ham."

"No, ma'am. The eggs and biscuits are filling enough. Thank you kindly."

Mina found Jack Johnson watching her and held her breath for a question about her wellbeing. It never came, so she exhaled, sat, and took a bite of her food. She relaxed as the men continued to discuss provisions Jack might want to take.

"I know Toby won't mind if you bring some dried fruit, extra flour, and coffee. It's basic. How are you with that?"

Jack grinned. "I've been blessed these last few years with time in cities, but I'm used to basic—grew up that way—and live that way when I'm work. It sounds like where I need to be for a couple of months."

Uncle Silas shared a look with her. Mr. Johnson had no idea about the harshness of the mountains.

"We will watch the weather for you. The temperature is dropping more this week. My bones tell me we are in for a deep, bitter cold before the first day of December. Getting snowed in up there might keep you from coming back to town a little longer than you plan," Silas said.

Jack shrugged. "I'll leave the Good Lord in charge of that. This is the first opportunity I've had to have time like this."

"The mountains are much different in the winter, Mr. Johnson. Old Toby is an excellent trapper and mountaineer. If he wasn't there, I'd find it ill-advised to let you go there," Mina said.

Jack rose and retrieved the coffee pot from the stove. He refilled everyone's cups before she realized his intention. "I am respectful of the mountain environment and want Toby to teach me. It's foolish not to listen. However, my travels have held other perils and trials. Perhaps the combination will help me survive."

Uncle Silas chuckled. "Not to worry, my boy. There are now other cabins a few miles from ours. It will be fine. Toby prepares well for the winter, but we'll be sure you have enough extra provisions. The sky looked a mite snowy this morning and as I said, my bones are aching. We might get an early one. I think you're wise to take the train from Golden to Georgetown and rent a mule and horse there. We did that when we took Daniel for a visit. It's quicker."

Bevil lifted his cup for Jack to fill. He took a sip and said, "Let me say this on Jack's behalf—if he's anything like his brother, and the others I served with during the war— he'll learn what he doesn't know pretty fast. I found *those* Arkansas men full of resourcefulness."

Jack smiled but said nothing. Mina wondered what mischief lurked behind that smile.

"Be careful, Jack. My visit there told me enough, and I stayed only a couple of days. It's primitive for a city boy like me," Daniel said.

"True, Nephew," Silas said. Her uncle wiped his mouth with his napkin and tossed it on his plate. "Well, gentlemen, since you insist on traveling alone to Toby's, I'll go to the store with you and send you on your way. I'll send a letter with you, and you'll let my friend, Mark, accompany you from Georgetown. He knows Toby and the way to the cabin."

Jack took the coffee pot back to the stove and returned to his seat. "Then it's settled."

He smiled at her, and Mina's heart raced.

The second knock of the day sounded at the door. Mina rose, grateful for the reprieve, and found Frank on the top step. She pulled him inside. He kicked the door closed, shutting out the cold air.

"Mina, what are you doing up and about?"

The sight of Frank filled Mina with relief and giddiness. She gave him a playful shove. "I'm not sick or harmed. That's better than you fared, my friend." Mina touched the bruising around his eye. He made a face at her and touched her bruised jaw.

"My pride and vanity are hurt more than my face. I am so sorry, Mina. I failed you."

"Why blame yourself? You had no way to anticipate it. Mr. Mathias distracted us with his departure. The man who injured you and took me, jumped us without warning."

Frank dropped his head. He scuffed the toe of his shoe on the floor and cut his eyes up at her. "Even so,

I've worked in rowdy places, Mina. I know how to fight."

"Please cease with this. I'm fine." She took his hand. "Come meet our guests."

Mina made introductions and hid a smile when Jack and Frank shook hands with measured regard.

Frank turned to her. "So, this is the Jack Johnson your uncle met all those years ago?"

"It is," she said.

"I am," Jack said.

Mina fought a smile. No one could deny the man's impressive stature. Too bad she'd never be able to impress him. Without warning, she started to shake. Tears started. She backed toward the door in horror as Frank and Jack both reached for her. Daniel intercepted them and reached her first. She took his arm and steadied herself.

"Gentlemen, I think we all need to be on our way. I need to check on a few patients," Daniel said.

Mina watched them don their coats. She released Daniel's arm as her composure returned. He grabbed his coat and joined Silas and Bevil at the door. They filed out the door with Jack last. He turned at the door.

"Nice meeting you, Frank. Take care of yourself, Miss Kolek."

Mina's heartbeat quickened again. What must he think of her? Why all his efforts on her behalf and such kind regard? She did not want his pity, but heaven help her, she still wanted his friendship. "It's *Mina*, Jack."

Mina approached him with outstretched hands, not daring to look at his face. After a brief delay, she felt his hands grasp hers. She raised her eyes to meet his. "Thank you for all you did for me, Jack."

Jack's astonished face took on a gentle expression. Tears misted her eyes.

He released her hands. "You're welcome, Mina. I better go now."

Mina nodded and stood at the door as he descended the stairs.

Jack turned on the bottom step and tipped his hat. She raised her hand and watched him mount his horse.

Mina sighed and shut the door. Frank laughed, bringing a crimson tint to her cheeks.

"I thought you found him irritating," Frank said.

"I *did*. I don't know, Frank." Mina turned and leaned against the door.

"Mina, are you okay?" Frank rushed to her, but she waved him away. He laughed. "I know better than to hover over you. You've never liked it. Anyway, Jack's got a firm handshake and looked me in the eye. It shows he's got character."

Mina grabbed a small lace pillow off the chair and collapsed on the mahogany framed sofa.

"He confuses me. I'm beginning to think I've sorely misjudged the man."

Frank pulled up a knee as he sat and faced her, both in comfortable postures reminiscent of many childhood conversations.

"Mina, in all your ponderings about the wayward young man Silas described to us as youths, what captured your fancy? I heard the story too, but my fifteen-year-old ears found nothing unusual."

Mina's blue eyes remained unguarded against her friend's probing gaze.

"I don't know, Frank. Maybe, the fact my uncle sensed something in him, enough to advise him. Uncle

Silas used to be a strict believer in minding your own business."

"That's true," Frank said. He stood, taking on one of her uncle's affectations. "When I asked Mr. Kolek what he thought of the theater, he said, 'Don't know enough about it. A man must tread his own road.'—or words close to that." Frank stroked his chin like Uncle Silas until Mina laughed. He joined in and returned to his seat beside her.

"I never did tell you about my trip to Arkansas." She adjusted in her seat to face him. "Daniel and I arrived just as Jack returned home after years away, only to discover his father died. Will, one of his brothers, did not welcome his return, whereas, his oldest brother seemed happy to have him. From what I learned, they both wanted to marry Alice Cushman as youths. Will is the one who did."

"Then why would he mind Jack returning now?"

"Men confuse me more and more—," Mina stopped as unbidden images of the man who abducted her and Mr. Mathias flashed through her mind. She took a deep breath and willed the memories away. "Except for you, Frank." She forced a smile and took his hand. "I mean that as a compliment, and a fortunate young lady will find you one day. Anyway, Jack did not seem to understand it either. That's why they fought. It made me think less of Jack at the time. But now, I'm not sure if my impressions during those first few days and our train trip gave him proper consideration."

"He's a surveyor for the railroads?"

"Yes, why?"

"Well, there's plenty of work for years to come, and after the railroads build all their tracks, there's bridges, towns, land lines for him to help establish. I'm sure Arkansas might also offer him many situations, but—"

"You think Colorado has more opportunities?"

"Colorado is young in its statehood and is changing with the railroad expansion. Even beyond that, are opportunities in Wyoming and Montana," Frank said.

"That is, if he wants to stay. He plans to winter with Toby. What he decides after that is up to him," she said.

"Give him a reason or at least something to think about while he's at the old cabin."

Mina nibbled on a fingernail and her eyes widened. She sat up straight and twisted toward her friend.

"Wait, Frank. I said I'd misjudged him is all. That doesn't mean anything more."

A skeptical lift of his eyebrows preceded his surrender.

"Very well, Mina. Anyway, maybe the time with Toby will help him decide," Frank said. He made one of his comical faces at her. "Enough. I've heard too much about the mythical Jack through the years. We've now met the real Jack. He's an ordinary man, just like me."

Mina giggled until Frank took her hand. His voice lost any tinge of humor. "What I want to know is—if you were hurt while they held you in one of the less savory establishments?"

"No," Mina said. She lifted her chin. "At least Mr. Mathias's orders kept the man from raping me."

"Mina!"

"You wondered, as I'm sure everyone in town has, Frank. I'd appreciate your help if possible. But it really doesn't matter. I know the truth."

"I'll do my best," Frank said. He released her hand

and stretched before readjusting against the back of the sofa. "Anyway, my father is better. I received a telegram the other day from a theater in Chicago. Looks like your friend may move to the big city. The head of the theater watched me perform in Montana."

Mina clasped her hands in delight. "Oh, Frank. How wonderful for you!" She grabbed the pillow and once again scooted back and down in her seat.

"You have my sincere appreciation for those words. My parents aren't sure about the advisability of such a move." Frank smiled and scooted down beside her. "I'll miss you, Mina. You're like a sister and best friend."

Mina laughed and threw the small pillow at him; her eyes appreciated his high cheekbones, blond hair, and blue eyes.

"No one but me knows a tough hunter and trapper lurk behind that handsome face. I'm glad our childhoods taught us to survive in the wild, while our older years have prepared us to also make our way in the city."

Frank turned his head to meet her gaze. "So am I, Mina. If you ever need me, I'll leave and come home."

"The same is true for me, Frank. When do you leave?"

Frank turned his head and strummed his fingers on the arm of the sofa. After a moment, he faced her and gave her nose a couple of playful taps. "Next week. They want me to leave before the weather turns too severe."

A smile spread on Mina's face, even as tears sprang to her eyes. She hugged him, blinking back the tears as she pulled away. "I'm really happy for your good fortune, but I'll miss you. It's earlier than I expected.

Your plans to stay here until spring pleased me, but I'll adjust. Are your parents, especially your father, able to handle things now?"

Frank reached in his pocket and found his handkerchief. He handed it to her. "Yes, in fact, your cousin's care has turned his health for the better. Even with their reservations about the theater profession, they know no one can afford to bypass opportunities."

Mina dabbed her eyes and blew her nose.

"You must go and succeed, Frank. There's only one favor before you go."

Frank gave a loosened strand of her hair an affectionate tug. "I miss your braids.

Mina made a face. Frank laughed.

"Very well, Mina. I'll do anything for you. What is it?"

"Go to church with me on Sunday." She clasped both of his hands in hers. "Please, please go—ignore the town gossips. Betsy and her family always sit with us. She says her parents are adamant about not changing anything."

"Done," Frank said. "And my parents will come, even though they are Methodists. Your church will host new visitors."

"Thank you, Frank, and my best to your parents for their kindness."

"Mina, they feel like you are one of theirs."

The sound of the front door opening interrupted them.

"Mrs. Simpson is gone," Daniel said. He shut the door behind him with a heavy sigh and removed his coat and hat. "Her lungs were too weak to fight the pneumonia. So Miss O'Connor said the office is quiet this morning and advised me to get a little rest before the afternoon."

After he hung his coat and hat on the hooks by the door, Daniel rubbed his face before his bloodshot eyes focused on them.

"What's wrong, Mina?"

Mina sniffed and wiped her nose again. She stood. "Nothing, in fact it's wonderful news. Frank is moving to Chicago. I'm sad because he might leave this week."

Frank stood and Daniel shook his hand.

"Congratulations. I'll write my family and give you their address. If you need anything, please call on them," Daniel said.

"That is kind. I appreciate it, Dr. Cummings. Now, if you will excuse me, I need to go. Mina, I'll see you Sunday morning. No need to see me to the door."

"Thank you, Frank," Mina said.

Weariness and immense sadness settled upon Mina when her friend shut the door. Tears spurted once again, and she stomped her foot.

Daniel's eyes narrowed and he came over to her.

"Mina, these emotional outbursts are due to the trauma you suffered. It is against your nature and frustrates you, but you must take extra care now. I want you to go rest for a few hours. You are not to return to work for a few more days."

"But—"

Daniel held up one of his hands. "No arguments."

Mina nodded.

~

Sunday morning proved less difficult than anticipated. The presence of her family and close friends insulated her from the stares and whispers.

141

Gratitude filled her when their pastor's opening prayer held thanksgiving for her restoration to her family without any harm.

Mina knew he'd stopped by and visited with her uncle and cousin after her ordeal. In this simple prayer, he conveyed to the congregation that her virtue remained in place. It bolstered her.

Then Mina bowed her head in silent prayer.

Dear Heavenly Father,

Please forgive me for caring so much about what people might think of me. I shouldn't need their approval but find myself desperately wanting it. Please help me to treasure Your approval above everyone else's. You know the truth and I know the truth—that's what matters. I'll not solicit the town's approval. But, if You see fit to send further affirmation, I'll be grateful. Still, regardless of what anyone else may say, I will walk forward. Your judgement is what counts. Please keep reminding my heart over my head, Lord.

In Jesus's Name–Amen.

Once finished, Mina refused to glance to the left or the right. Her focus remained on the sermon throughout the rest of the service.

Mina breathed a sigh of relief at the well wishes and polite nods present as they left the church service. A second prayer of thankfulness overtook her on the ride home. She smiled as Daniel helped her from the buggy. The thought of her return to work without ado the next day filled her with happiness.

Chapter Fourteen

The cold snow at the higher altitude invigorated Jack. He had adjusted to the heights, and his breathing no longer became short during his chores.

Toby taught him much about the mountain-man way of life. His exaggerated stories held enough truth to garner respect. The man demonstrated excellent trapping and hunting skills beyond the ones Jack already knew.

Jack inhaled the brisk chill and exhaled his warmed breath, watching it turn into frosty smoke. The insulation from his two-month beard and the fur hat he wore every day provided welcome protection. The musty, warm smell of pelts comforted and no longer repelled him.

Jack squinted at the line of trees, searching for Toby. The old man should have returned by now.

The rustle of branches, scattering snow near the edge of white barked trees where he'd last seen Toby held his scrutiny. Soon, Toby's bulky form emerged, followed by two more people. They led a pack mule and two horses. Jack frowned and tromped through the snow toward them.

The man behind Toby jerked off his cap and waved it at him. Jack smiled and waved back at Silas Kolek. His heart quickened, searching the slight, but well layered form next to Silas. He drew his conclusion and waved again.

"Look who I found," Toby said.

Jack removed his hat.

"What brings you way out here, Silas?"

The smaller, more feminine form, even in britches, reached inside her coat.

"We brought your mail, Mr. Johnson."

Jack licked his parched, snow burned lips and took the packet of letters she held.

"Thank you, Miss Kolek. Remember, it's Jack."

"Is it?" Mina's eyes twinkled. "Well, I wanted to be sure, Jack. I don't think I'd have known you with a beard."

Jack rubbed the wiry bristles. "My pa always kept a beard. I wanted to try it, and it's served me well in this snow."

Toby shook his head. He took the reins of the pack mule and Mina's horse. "Let's get these animals into the shed. Do we have stew ready?"

"Yes, Toby, I made it and set it by the hearth before I left to check on you," Jack said.

"No need. I always arrive directly," Toby said. "You get Mina inside."

"Yes, sir."

Silas and Toby headed toward the shed with the horses and mule in tow.

The isolation and intimacy of the snow covered

foothills and mountain valley seemed to increase once the older men left them. It unnerved Jack in Mina's presence. He swept his arm toward the cabin. "This way, ma'am."

Mina laughed. She studied the still distant peaks above them. "I grew up here—except for my travels with Uncle Silas on his various jobs before I went to town at fifteen. The cabin hasn't moved." She strode ahead of him.

"Of course," Jack mumbled.

Jack and Mina stomped the snow off their boots beside the door and entered. Once inside, they removed their layers of coats.

Jack grabbed the handle of the pot beside the hearth and returned it to the hook, swinging the iron arm back over the flames.

"It'll get hot again real soon."

Mina pulled the pot back toward the outer hearth again. She picked up the wooden spoon, stirred the stew, and tasted it.

"Hmmm, I am impressed. It's actually quite edible."

Jack laughed. He reached around her and repositioned the pot over the steady flames. "Thank you, Mina."

Mina placed the spoon on the roughhewn table and gestured to the packet of mail he'd laid there. "Aren't you going to read your correspondence? I believe there's a letter from your brother."

Jack understood more about Mina after stilted, but informative conversations with Toby, but her lack of curtesy and blunt ways still astounded him. He stared at her. "You went through my letters?"

Mina's parched cheeks reddened even more. She

lifted her hand and started to bite on a fingernail but dropped her hand and stepped away from him instead.

"No—the one on top is from Arkansas," Mina said.

Jack slid off the letter from the top of the stack. The familiar penmanship of his oldest brother proved her right.

"It's from Marc." He laid it aside and reached back to retrieve the rest of the small bundle, thumbing through the other four; he picked out the one from his boss at the Union-Pacific Railroad. It thanked him for his recent assistance and proposed continued opportunities, as well as notification of his awaiting payments for his job in Fort Collins. The next came from the courthouse in Hot Springs concerning planned city works projects within their city and surrounding county. The bottom letter held updates on events in Texas from his brother's, and now also his, dear friend, Boyd Richards.

Jack loved those rare moments when he caught Mina watching him. He'd thought about her. No conclusions, but—he loved those moments.

She ducked her head and retrieved the simple tin plates from the wooden shelf over the washbasin. She stepped around him. "I better set the table."

Mina placed each plate and whirled to pass him again.

The tension suffocated Jack. He placed a hand on her arm. "Mina."

Mina's eyes lingered on his hand. He jerked his hand away in embarrassment.

"Yes, Jack?"

"Would you read Marc's letter with me?"

Confusion registered in Mina's eyes, and she

blinked a few times.

"You want me to read your brother's letter *with* you? Why?"

Jack's ponderings over the last couple of months made an honest answer the best. He'd wrestled with God and himself over the situation with Will. He'd even solicited advice from Toby a bit, but the mountain man listened more than talked. The old man liked *to do* more than philosophize. Jack learned much from the man but knew he never wanted to live such an isolated life. He wanted to find love again, and he wanted to be close to family. Still, he didn't know how close he could live to them with Will's feelings on the matter. Will had not responded to his letter before he left Denver and there wasn't one from him in this bundle. At least Marc had written.

"I have no idea if Marc's letter is full of simple news or life changing family events, but I trust you to give an honest reaction, in contrast to my very biased and emotion-shaded view."

Mina's eyes held his.

"I am flattered, Jack, but it is your family not mine."

"Please, Mina."

The sound of boots outside of the door broke the intimacy present in the cabin. Miners and mountain men cared little about social propriety, but Jack still respected their situation and turned away from her.

As the door opened, Jack felt her pat his shoulder. He turned and she gave him a brief nod before retrieving cups for the coffee.

Their midday meal passed with updates on the store, politics, and Daniel's practice and recent engagement to his nurse, Miss O'Connor.

"Daniel is enjoying being in Colorado instead of Chicago at this time. He is able to avoid the long courtship his parents might expect," Mina said.

Jack chuckled. Toby grunted.

"I'm sure he does. When is the wedding and how do her parents feel?" Jack said.

"Shannon and Daniel plan to be married in Ft. Collins in April. Her parents live there and are excited. Daniel wrote a letter to request their blessing last month."

Jack turned to Silas. His friend remained quiet on this particular subject. "What do you think?"

Silas took a sip of coffee and propped his elbows on the table. "I think they're well matched. They've made up their minds about each other. How 'bout you, Jack? Have you made any decisions?"

Jack glanced at Mina. Her eyes met his before he turned back to respond.

"Well, I'm close, Silas. The letters you brought will help confirm my thoughts or make me re-think things again. It seems I have confirmed job situations in both Colorado and Arkansas. I hoped to have a response from Will, but I guess Marc's letter will tell me what I need to know."

Silas blew on the steaming coffee in his cup. "Why haven't you read it?"

"Uncle Silas, he hasn't had time," Mina said. She stood to clear their plates. "He read his business ones first, as is prudent. He'll read it. Jack, do you mind helping me get a couple of buckets of snow to melt for wash water?"

"My pleasure, ma'am," Jack said.

Once outside, Mina led him a few yards from the cabin to a deep snowdrift against a clump of large rocks. She set the buckets down and sat on one of the rocks, patting the other for him. Realization settled. He assessed and pulled her back to her feet.

"Jack—"

"Wait, Mina. If we are to read this letter together, I think it's best for me to sit, and you read it over my shoulder. That way, if your uncle comes, we are appropriate."

"Thank you," she said.

He sat, and she circled behind him. Jack took the envelope from his pocket, opened it, and unfolded the pages:

Dear Jack,

I received your letter the week after Will received his. My hope to find him relenting waned, as our brother is stubborn and prideful.

Out of curiosity, I asked him if he would feel differently if he'd won the fight. He allowed it might have put salve to his pride but nothing changes your deserting him. That's what he thinks, Jack. He wanted you to come home, concede in graciousness, congratulate Alice and him, and find a local girl to marry here—but you left.

He says you both knew Alice could only choose one of you. You each promised to be gentlemen about it when the time came. He thinks you broke your promise, Jack. It's hard for him to understand your difficulties.

I told him young boys made that pact. In a way, you did the most gentlemanly thing. You allowed them to build a life without the guilt from seeing you each day.

He said you could have come home after your first work with the railroad instead of returning to the university in Missouri. Then, he wouldn't have insisted Florey and I come home when Pa first became ill.

Jack, that is unfounded. As I told you, as the eldest, that duty lay with me.

Will saved the farm. That is true.

We both made choices that took us away.

However, as I reminded him, God's plans are more important. Everything happened with a purpose beyond our own.

His bitterness will destroy not only him, but also Alice and his precious children.

I read your letter to him. It chilled me to know how your words did not soften his heart. Therefore, as the eldest brother, I've made a decision—one our ma supports. It is time Will travels away from here to see a bit of the country and challenges in your life. Alice delivered her baby, so she will remain here.

By the time you receive this letter, Ma and our stubborn brother should arrive in Denver within a few days of this letter. Our family and church have contributed to their travel expenses.

I trust you will arrange for their winter visit once they arrive. Our family has stood together through too much to remain divided. Even my poor decisions after the war found forgiveness here. Will owes you no less.

Your brother,

Marc

Post Script: Please tell Bevil Henry I am pleased you've met. He was a good soldier and a true friend to Matt.

Jack stood so fast that Mina pitched forward, but he

caught her as he whirled.

"I'm sorry, Mina. It's just—"

"You need to get back to Denver, Jack," she said. "It takes at least two days. Be thankful for the train once we get to Georgetown or it would take longer. It's too late to start today."

"Did you camp on your way here, Mina? Bevil and I did for a night."

Mina shook her head. "Uncle Silas knows better than that with the weather the way it is. We went a little out of the way to stay with friends. Jack, if they arrive while we're gone, Daniel will take care of them. This is not the time to travel. We planned to stay a few days, but, if the weather holds, we can leave in the morning."

Jack scanned the sky. "More snow is due."

"Jack, you will get back to Denver when the Good Lord allows it. This weather might have presented delays for them too."

Jack shut his eyes for a moment of silent prayer. He opened his eyes and smiled. "You're right, Mina. Thank you."

Jack grabbed a pail and bent to scoop the deep snow. Mina did likewise with the other pail, but when she straightened, a spray of snow hit him in the face.

Shock and humor coursed through Jack as he emptied his pail in her direction. Mina gasped and laughed. The sound captivated him. He wiped his face on his sleeve, mesmerized.

"I like it when you're happy. Your eyes are sparkling like stars," Jack said. A tenderness he'd never known gripped his heart. His gaze mingled with hers. *This is not what she needs.* He turned away and retrieved and refilled the pails.

"Thank you." Mina said. She smiled once he straightened. "You did say you wanted my opinion on the letter. Most men wouldn't ask for a woman's opinion."

"I know, but they aren't me, and we're not in public. The mountains and I welcome your thoughts, Mina."

She reached for one of the pails and clasped it in front of her with both hands on the handle.

"It seems your big brother has taken the reins long enough to move you to a place of neutrality. Denver is not your home, nor is it Will's. No matter what Will wants, where you decide to settle is up to you. It does give your brother the opportunity to consider the life you've led. His conclusions will be his own. So, neither one of you can control the opinions of the other. Keep that in mind when you see him."

"That's so. It's just—"

"Now, from what I've observed of you—you consider other people before yourself at this point in life. Once, you were a hurt young man with selfish disappointment. Although I initially misjudged you, you've matured. In retrospect, it's noticeable in how you interacted with Alice and even in leaving to give your brother more time after your brawl. The fight is your one regret if you're honest."

"True," Jack said. Her astute assessment amazed him. "Please continue."

"In my opinion, this visit gives Will the chance to forgive. Still, that's up to him alone. For you, I want you to focus on your mother. She is now a widow. Pray for God to help you see her needs. I know your brothers see to her material needs, but women have many emotional needs they don't discuss. Simple gestures and time spent together are often the most treasured. Every mother wants to feel valued and needed—that's what I've observed. She took care of all of you and due to the war, learned early about entrusting her children to God's care in all things. Now that she's older, it's time for her children to consider and honor her. Don't focus on Will; let God work on his heart. Open yours to your mother—look to helping her." She closed the few snowy feet between them and took his hand.

He could see the earnestness in her face, so he waited.

"That's my opinion—the opinion of one motherless daughter—as one who treasures mothers. I trust you to pray about it and decide." Mina turned in the direction of the cabin.

Realization filled Jack. He watched her, needing to ask the question plaguing him ever since he left Denver.

"Mina. Wait."

She turned. His boots found the smaller prints of hers in the snow on his way to join her.

"You've helped me, and not that you asked for my thoughts, but I wanted to find out how you're feeling about your kidnapping ordeal now. Will you ever consider marriage?"

She searched his face. "Jack, I want to apologize—"

"Mina, no, no—that's not why I asked. It's not about me. I understand your turning down my foolish, but sincere proposal. You're smart." Jack said, flashing a grin. She didn't smile. So he continued. "No, it's—I think we're friends, or at least, I hope we are, and I wanted you to be able to talk to me. I mean, I know you've talked to Betsy and Frank. They know your heart, so pouring out your ordeal to them makes more sense. It might seem untoward to discuss things with me. I don't know."

"I did talk to them, just not about everything. What happened is *not* proper, and I can only imagine Betsy's mortification."

The pit of Jack's stomach lurched in trepidation. "Did more happen to you than—?"

Her eyes glimmered with tears. She blinked and pulled down the brim of her hat before releasing a torrential flow of words.

"Not like that, no, not physically. I mean the loathsome man put his hands all over me. If Miss Lily hadn't entered the room, my shame would—well, you know." Mina ducked her head for a moment. "Nevertheless, Jack, I've told God everything, and I've read the Bible throughout this time. Things of deep consequence happen in that brothel." She lifted her chin. "As it seems words fly out of my mouth on subjects men and women do not discuss in polite conversation, I guess it's time for me to say things aloud. If I shock you, *you* asked, and God knows my thoughts."

What had he done? Still, he did ask her and *did* care. He led her back to the rock and dusted off the snow so she could sit, while he stood.

"Please, go on, Mina."

She adjusted the brim of her hat and her eyes met his. "You know how God took a rib out of Adam and made Eve?"

There she went. Jack *had* asked. He tried not to frown in his confusion, but could not refrain from asking her to clarify. "Yes, but how does that apply here, Mina?"

"Well, I think men are always searching for the missing part."

Unease mixed with intrigue kept him silent. He waited and she continued.

"I don't really understand all about it, but it seems to me that God always intended a reunion and sanctioned it in marriage. Whenever men and women seek it outside of marriage, they lose even more of themselves, because they never become whole. Instead, they fracture their souls." Her voice dropped to a whisper. "At least that would explain what I—it shattered part of me just observing it."

Tears coursed down her face under the shadow of the hat. Jack wanted to comfort her, but knew he shouldn't try.

She managed a brief glance at him before she resumed in a shaky but audible voice. "The emotionally fractured women I saw in the mining camps wore this shattered expression. As a child, I never forgot it. The women who entered the room where they kept me had it. The haunted look left during— but it returned— after." She frowned and sought his gaze as if seeking a glimpse into his soul. "I did not see it in the men—the man who grabbed me put a knife to my throat and made me watch until I challenged him to kill me, and Miss Lily intervened." She released an unsteady breath. "Anyway, I suspect, there is a hardening of their hearts and a callous disregard forming within. Depending on how fractured each person is before they marry, these things may also be present in marriages. After my friend in Chicago died, I suspected this and now feel it's true. Also, I think you must trust the person."

Her eyes met his and a flash of unwarranted guilt churned. He shifted his weight but refused to look away as she continued.

"It is very serious. I am no longer naïve and, if I'm honest, I'm scared. My ordeal made me more resolute than ever to wait for a man who can share my life in the way God intended."

She glanced up at Jack.

Jack closed his mouth and swallowed. He stroked his bearded face before sitting on the rock beside hers. Jack removed his hat and stared straight ahead. He took care not to look at her when he spoke.

"Mina, my parents had, and my brothers and their wives have what you want in a marriage. I've also known people God's healed and forgiven of their pasts. His redemption made marriage possible for them. You've pondered it to a level everyone should, but few do, especially men. They are consumed by the physical and don't think on the rest. I've suffered the temptation but am glad I refrained." He turned his head toward her. "You are unlike any woman I've ever met, Mina." He slapped his hat against his knee. "I want to make the man who snatched you pay even more than Mathias. I'm outraged. And in this case, I do have anger issues, and I'm not apologizing for it." She lifted her head and shifted to face him. Their eyes met. He softened his voice. "I can't imagine how devastated you felt. Forgive my gall at proposing to you in such a situation, and thank you for stepping on my pride. Someone needed to." He stood, taking the buckets in one hand. "The cold is seeping through my coat. It's time to get you inside."

~

It took a day more than planned to get back to Denver due to the weather. Jack learned more about the communities of Idaho Springs, Georgetown, and all the sparse cabin occupants in between from Silas's narrative as they traveled. He also discovered things about Mina. She never complained about the journey and never showed fear, but when she slept, the determination ebbed. Her tossing woke him during the night at Toby's cabin. Silas shook his head and told him to go back to sleep, but he couldn't. Her uncle tucked a blanket around her, her eyes flickered open, and her breathing calmed at the sight of the old man. When Jack asked Silas about it, he said these "nerves of the night" started before she came to him, calmed and disappeared for a few years, but reemerged when he started his travels without her. They disappeared again—until after her ordeal with Mathias.

They arrived at Dr. Cummings and the Kolek's home after dusk on Saturday. The smells in the city now seemed sour compared to the freshness of the mountain air. Mina laughed when he wrinkled his nose.

Silas shook his head at them, climbed out of the wagon, and stretched his back with a few popping vertebrae. He turned toward the man with the reins in his hands. "I'm glad you were at the depot, especially with the delay, Charlie. Thanks for bringing us home."

The man shook his head. "Glad to help, Silas. This weather delays people and freight. I had to be there and my route takes me by here anyway. Do you need help with your things?"

Silas shook his head as Jack tossed down their bedrolls and combined baggage.

Jack helped Mina from the wagon and turned to

look up at Charlie. "Wait, I'll go on to the hotel," he said.

"No, Jack. It's Saturday and many people are in town. The rooms may be full. You can bunk with me," Silas said.

The cold weariness from the day settled on him.

"Thank you. I'll go help Charlie with his load. It's the least I can do for his trouble. You and Mina go on up to bed," Jack said.

Charlie smiled. "I appreciate this, Mr. Johnson. I might even have time to stop off for a drink before bed."

The noise from the saloons and still active streets engaged his mind after so much time in pristine isolation. The topography of the area in Denver seemed such a contrast now. Jack liked both, but he knew he'd never live like Toby. He marveled that Silas and Mina once did. A month or two during the year—like his recent respite—restored a person. The hills, rocks, and skies didn't mind his wails of grief for his father. A natural cathedral of snowy earth and blue sky shared the reverence of his prayers each day. He liked Toby and respected the man's reticence. Surveyors enjoyed working outside, but they also liked office time and interactions. Jack liked his work.

The small amount of freight didn't take long to unload. Jack enjoyed his walk back through town. He noticed Daniels' buggy remained absent from its familiar spot in front of the office. He must still be out on a call or at the hospital. The dimly lit windows at the still early evening hour did not alarm him as he climbed the stairs. He found the door unlocked and a single lamp on the kitchen table. Silas and Mina must have gone straight to bed.

Jack left both his smelly fur hat and coat by the door and headed to Silas's room. He scratched at his beard and resolved to rise early enough to shave before church the next morning. A complete bath—he yawned. The blanket-covered man in the bed emitted a series of loud snores. Silas must be tired; he did not snore during their journey. Jack removed his boots and clothes with extra care not to disturb Silas. Still, the mattress creaked on the supporting ropes when he eased under the covers and turned on his side with his back toward the sleeping man.

The snores dissipated and Jack ginned until he felt the distinctive prick of a knife tip at the back of his neck.

"You're not old enough to be the owner of this bed. So, you're either an unannounced guest or a drunken man who wandered in by mistake," the man wielding the knife said.

Exasperation, at the sound of the familiar voice, accompanied the well-placed elbow he placed in the man's ribs. He jumped out of the bed before the man applied the knife blade.

"*Will*, it's me," he said, just as the stocky figure sprang from the bed and slammed him against the door. Jack grunted and held his breath as he felt the knife blade against his throat.

His brother's face moved closer to his in the darkness. "Jack?"

"Yes, didn't Silas and Mina tell you?"

Will stepped back, dropping his arms. "No, I haven't seen them. I went to bed right after the doctor left on his call this afternoon. We got here right after lunch. Train travel delays plagued us the whole journey."

Jack rubbed his throat.

"You boys all right?" Silas asked outside the door.

Jack opened the door. "Yeah, my brother thought he'd jumped a bandit or a drunk."

Lamplight appeared behind Silas, illuminating Mina and his mother.

Silas took the lamp. "Mina, you go back to bed. The men aren't dressed."

Jack avoided looking at Mina, but laughed at the look on his mother's face before she pushed past Silas and threw herself at him. Mina's words of advice came back to him. He hugged his mother before she reared back to look at him.

"Jack, how could anyone recognize you with that wild beard? You do resemble your pa a bit, but he kept his trimmed. I am shaving you in the morning."

"Ma, I'm happy to see you, too."

She wrinkled her nose. "You stink; probably worse than your brother. I managed to bathe before I went to bed. Mina also freshened up a bit. Travel is not kind, but I guess women mind it a bit more than you men."

"I'll go to the hotel early in the morning and take care of cleaning up a bit before church." Jack kissed his mother's cheek. "Please go back to bed. Daniel's had a long day and shouldn't walk in on this. He needs to come home to a sleeping house."

"Jack and Will, look at me." Their mother did not move until they complied. She put her hands on her hips. "I expect both of you to also sleep. No bickering. Everything else can wait until in the morning."

His brother grunted and crawled back into bed. Jack

took notice when he reached under his pillow for his knife sheath. He released his breath as Will slid the knife in the cover and laid it on the bedside table.

Their mother smiled. "Good night, Jack."

She stopped in front of Silas. "Mr. Kolek, please forgive my less than proper state."

Silas Kolek inclined his head and stood back for her to pass. "Not at all, Mrs. Johnson. Rest well."

"Good night," she said.

The door to Mina's room closed, and Silas shook his head.

"Jack, I'm sorry for not warning you. Your ma greeted us when we opened the door. She told me Daniel gave Will my room for the night, so I planned to share with Daniel. Thought you two could sort things out amongst yourselves."

Jack laid a hand on Silas's shoulder. "It's fine, and we did." He grinned. "In our own fashion."

Silas rubbed his beard. "Good night, Jack." He shut the door.

Jack slid into the bed. "No more snoring, Will."

His brother tugged on the blanket. "No, yanking covers, Jack."

Jack grinned and flipped on his side, pulling the blanket with him. The expected response tug soon followed. Weariness soon stilled both of them.

Jack heard Daniel shuffle into his room in the wee hours. As tired as he was, sleep eluded him after Daniel's arrival, so he got up and put on his clothes. Will turned when he picked up his boots. His brother sat up, wiping his eyes.

"Where are you going at this hour?"

"The hotel. I need to get a bath and arrange for

rooms for tonight. I also left a few of my things in storage there."

"What makes you think anyone will be awake?"

"There's always someone," Jack said.

"Mind if I go with you?"

Jack's insides tightened. Well, they *must* talk about things. "Sure. Be quiet. We can put our boots on outside, so we don't wake up everyone."

His stocky brother bumped into a few things in the small room, dressing in haste. It reminded him of the times they'd slipped out of their room to go hunting early.

Jack held his breath until they closed the front door and took a new, lung-chilling one. He didn't take another one until they reached the bottom of the stairs.

"We'll catch our death out here. This reminds me of the snow dropped on us at home last winter. I can't imagine it being a regular thing," Will said.

Jack shook his head. "You get used to many things if you're away from Arkansas long enough." He looked at the dim sky before he pulled out his pocket watch. "It's four. Follow me and keep your eyes open."

Jack adjusted his warm hat and took long, quick strides, thankful to find the streets quiet.

A man stepped out of the shadows a few buildings from the hotel. Jack recognized him.

"Good morning, Deputy."

The man stared at him without a flicker of recognition.

"It's Jack Johnson. I met you a couple of months ago."

The man peered at him. "You sure don't look the same. Who's this with you?"

"William Johnson, my brother from Arkansas. He arrived with my mother yesterday. Mr. Kolek and his niece fetched me from old Toby's."

The deputy nodded. "Well, I better warn you. Mr. Mathias is still in town. The police jailed him and his accomplice until the trial last week, but the jury didn't see that any lasting harm came of it, so he's free. It's a shame. In the old days, before statehood, we had swift forms of territorial justice." He gave a meaningful wink. "I don't know anymore. I do my job. The chief of police and the sheriff all have a challenge now. Where are you headed?"

"The hotel."

The man sniffed at him. "Good idea, Johnson. Stay out of trouble."

"Yes, sir."

Will kept pace with him.

A cowboy held the door open for them on his way out of the hotel.

A Spanish woman carrying towels passed them in the lobby.

"Ma'am. *Baños? Lavarse*," Jack said.

"*Si'*, *senor*, you want a bath?"

Jack nodded, and after further explanation about the clothes he left there, she escorted them to a room with three tubs in it. She spoke to Will, but he shook his head.

"What did she say?"

"She wants to know if you also want a bath."

Will frowned but nodded.

"You can put back on your same clothes and change once we go back to the Koleks. I'm sorry mine won't fit you."

While they waited for the filling of the tubs, Jack dug through his bag the woman retrieved for him and found his straight razor and soap.

He poured water into the basin on the wooden stand, picked up his blade, peered up at the oval mirror over it, and began the tedious process of the removal of most of the beard before he applied soap for a shave.

Will watched him. "You want to tell me about that deputy?"

Jack shrugged and told him the whole story. He turned away from the mirror and pointed his shaving blade at his brother. "Wait and see—Mathias is still going to cause trouble at some juncture. Men like that always do. I'll let Silas know."

His brother shook his head. "How have you stayed alive?"

The question surprised Jack. He turned back and rinsed his razor in the basin bowl.

"Will, there are also hangings, killings, robberies, and such in Arkansas. You get used to the people and the way things are done. I've adjusted to watching people on a wider horizon and treat people as strangers until I'm sure of their friendship. Besides, when I'm working, the people involved are familiar to me. Surveyors don't carry payrolls. But I have dealt with a few complaints about claim disputes when we look at property lines."

The woman came in to finish preparations. After placing a towel and soap beside each tub, she left, shutting the door behind her.

Will removed his clothes and climbed into one of the steaming tubs.

"You'd better finish up there before your water gets

cold."

Jack observed the steam hovering over the tubs. "I think I'll be fine."

However, he did make short work of his last few swipes, nicking himself in the process. He scowled, and Will grinned.

After he settled into the tub next to his brother, the inevitable conversation started.

"I've resented you for not coming home for years and even hated you for it, Jack. After you"—Will rubbed his ribs— "dern near killed me with your fancy fighting, I was certain. But, I'm starting to think our big brother had it right."

Having read Marc's letter, Jack understood, but Will continued.

"Traveling all this way with Ma, seeing the people on the trains and at our stops, and even what I've seen here so far, makes me realize how much I don't know about you. But the thing that has bothered and frustrated me, even hurt me, is your lack of concern for your family or their feelings. Doesn't family mean anything to you anymore, Jack?"

Jack stared at him in stunned silence, leaned his head back against the tub and tried to swallow the lump of tears, pride, and self-defense lodged in his throat. He stared up at the ceiling and let his choked words of candor flow.

"I first left because Alice picked you, and I couldn't pretend it didn't matter—a pure childish and impulsive action on my part. Thank goodness, Silas Kolek told me to go home. He made me mad. I jumped on my horse and raced a few miles before turning toward home, but still I only went as far as Missouri.

"Once I got into the university, I loved my studies. The idea of travel and new possibilities took hold of me. Yes, it seems selfish in a way, but I also think it's what needed to happen. I *tried* to keep in touch with my letters home. Ma and Marc both answered my letters even though traveling kept those correspondences delayed. Pa never did much letter writing. That's why the one he left for me means even more." The words from the near memorized pages replayed in his mind. He stared at the steam rising from the now dingy water.

"Jack?"

The sound of Will's hand hitting the water registered just as the consequential splash hit Jack's arm over the side of the tub. He turned his head to meet Will's questioning gaze. "Reading Pa's letter gave me affirmation because he felt that too," he said. "But—I wish I'd come home before he died. I waited too late, and I can't take it back, Will."

Will nodded. "No, but we can get past this and honor him by it. Are you willing?"

Jack stared at his brother for a moment, not believing the olive branch offered. He'd prayed so hard for so long. He nodded and laughed. "How can I argue sitting here without a stitch on in this tub?"

Will chuckled. "This water is becoming less tolerable. We'd better have a quick scrub."

Within ten minutes, they finished and dressed.

The aroma of coffee, ham, and bacon wafted through the air from the restaurant.

"Let's have breakfast here. I'll check on rooms for us for the week."

Will scuffed the toe of his shoe against the front desk. "Our visit is just for few days, Jack. I've brought enough to provide for Ma and me."

Jack did not want to hurt his brother's pride. "I think it might be easier to get a single room for us and let Ma stay with the Koleks. I'd have one anyway. You can get breakfast if you'll let me treat you and Ma to a couple of meals this week."

"What if Miss Kolek and Ma cooked for us?"

"It's early; they might figure what we're about," Jack said.

Will glanced toward the rows of tables and chairs.

"It does smell good. I think it's time to see if Denver's grub is as good as Arkansas' is."

After finding a table, Will propped his elbows on it and leaned forward. "You know one of the things life's taught me? "

Jack waited.

"You don't really know how much life costs until you're paying for it—in money and responsibility. Children work with their parents as we did, but I'm now the one making sure we make it each day. Like Pa did for us and . . . and . . .," Will paused, swallowed hard, and continued, "how amazing wives and mothers are. Only when you've seen your wife giving birth, and especially when you've almost lost her in childbirth, do you start to understand."

Jack's eyes widened. He couldn't fathom it. "You almost lost Alice? When?"

Will's eyes clouded with pain. "It happened during the birth of our second child. No, not the one she delivered this December. Robert's birth was tough being her first, and it scared me a mite, but the second—something wasn't right, and the baby came early, and she started bleeding real bad—anyway, we lost him."

What? No! Jack's heart ached. The harsh reality of the missed years with his brother hit him. He leaned back, clearing his throat. "I'm sorry."

Will nodded, but allowed a sad smile that brightened as he talked.

"Yep. It never leaves you, but the Good Lord gave us Gabriel before Christmas without one problem for Alice."

Jack reached out his hand. "Congratulations, Will. I hope to meet little Gabriel one day."

Will shook his hand without hesitation. "How about going home with us?"

Jack placed his hands on the edge of the table. His thumbs rubbing the crisp tablecloth as he studied Will, who seemed in earnest. The Lord must have worked overtime on his brother. "You'd really want that? I mean you've earned your way—taking over everything."

"Well, Jack, I've also pondered some things since our fight. But it took me coming out here to really see things. I've been prideful. You may not know this, but if Marc hadn't come home when he did and taught me to quit thinking so much of myself, I might have lost the farm. I wouldn't listen to Pa or Ma and stayed determined to do it my way during his illness. Marc's experiences in Texas and the money he loaned me saved everything. But I've paid him back and learned a few lessons. Guess I still had another to learn about you. Train travel and city life bother *me*."

Jack lifted his eyebrow. "Really? It's always excited me until this past year. The work is what I should be doing. I get to be part of growing this country, Will."

"That's like you. Your enthusiasm for things always exceeded measure. But if you felt this way, why did you try and come home?" Will said.

"I've missed family," Jack said without hesitation. "Work only satisfies you for a while if you have a family like ours. Some men only have work."

Will reached into his coat pocket and pulled out an envelope. He tapped it on the table a couple of times. "Do you think surveying for the county is satisfying work?"

Jack's mouth went dry. He stared at the envelope. Hope glimmered. "Well, I've never done it to this point but sure wouldn't mind giving it a try. What's that?"

"The mayor came by the house and said he'd been to Hot Springs the week after you left. He said you'd impressed them during your visit to the courthouse and wanted to know if we'd send you this. He said it's an offer for work all over Hot Springs County if you're interested." Will held out the envelope. "Read over it and compare it to whatever they're offering you here. But don't let me be the reason for not coming home."

Absolution at last—Jack stared at his brother. He leaned back and glanced away. Other diners talked around them, oblivious to the significance of this moment for him. What would they do if he stood up and whooped? He turned his head. Or, what if he released the tears choking him? Instead, he shut his eyes for a moment.

Will cleared his throat.

Jack opened his eyes and took the offered envelope. "Thank you, Will." He held it for a moment before tucking it into his coat pocket.

The waitress brought coffee and they ordered. The

aroma from the steaming contents and the warmth of the cup in his hands calmed Jack's racing thoughts. All thoughts of work and plans left him.

Will set his cup on the table with a thump, sloshing the contents on the white tablecloth. He cocked his head to the side. "Let's have it, Jack."

"How do always know when my thoughts are shifting? You've always known," Jack said.

Will reached across to flick his ear. Then he pointed at Jack. "Learning the signs—you bite on one side of your bottom lip. Your quick changing thoughts often got us in trouble. Well?"

Awareness of the slight pain in his lower lip brought a smile. Jack laughed. "I guess I do chew it a bit." He lowered his cup to the table, keeping both hands around its warmth. "How's Ma doing, Will?"

"Well enough to make me feel about ten years old during the trip out here. I'll never take a train ride alone with her again unless all is well with the family. She'd given a few *soft* reprimands to me about you before, in contrast to Pa's and Marc's firm opinions. But, once she got me alone, away from Alice and the rest of the family, she returned to the candid and convincing woman who raised us. Sitting here with you brings every word she said back to me."

"What did she say?"

"She said she was glad you went with Uncle Samuel. It allowed Alice to decide which one of us she really loved. The greater tragedy would have been for you to marry Alice, only for her to find out she'd chosen the wrong brother."

That smarted a bit.

"She said that? How does she know?"

"Don't tell me you think otherwise, Jack?"

Pride puffed, but soon deflated within Jack. He traced the rim of the cup with his finger and shook his head. "No, I don't. I'm happy for you both."

Will readjusted his stocky form in the hard chair. "Good. Anyway, Ma pointed out how Marc going to war had taught her and Pa to let go of you more easily. At least they knew you weren't at war every day. The pain she felt during those war years only became bearable when she completely put Marc in God's hands. She did the same with you. They both wanted you to find your own path. It did not have to be my path. When she said that, I realized the truth of it. I grew up thinking you'd always be around. Marc's absence during those years made us closer. You were supposed to want the farm life like me, but you didn't, did you?"

"No, not really. I thought I did once. Then schooling and life in Missouri showed me opportunities beyond those at home. It's as it should be, Will. Now, back to Ma. Have you talked to her about her feelings since Pa died?"

"Not directly," Will said. "Alice and Florey have a bit. I've seen Marc just walk up and hug her without saying anything numerous times. Talking about it is not something she seems to want."

The waitress arrived with plates of ham, eggs, and fluffy biscuits. "Here you go, sirs.'

Jack moved his cup and sat back as she placed their plates in front of them. "Thank you, ma'am."

"I'll bring more coffee. Enjoy your breakfast." The waitress gave them a practiced smile and departed.

Jack picked up his fork. He scooped a bite of eggs

and held it suspended. "I want to talk to Ma, Will."

"You're welcome to try."

Jack ate the eggs off the fork, chewed, and took a bite of a warm biscuit. The light and fluffy bread tasted so much better than the ones he and Toby made.

Will cleared his throat

Jack forced himself to finish chewing and swallowed. "What?" He noticed his brother's fork remained on the table. "Oh." He bowed his head as his brother said grace.

Chapter Fifteen

The brothers' companionable bantering as they approached from the street surprised Mina almost as much as the discovery of their mother in her room last night. She tried to imagine Jack's shock when he found his brother in her uncle's room. After the ruckus following his discovery the previous night, she did not expect the jovial pair approaching the stairs where she stood. Mrs. Johnson told her the boys mended fences better when left alone—after a well-placed nudge.

Mina smiled. She and Mrs. Johnson made breakfast together. The wonderful woman taught her ways to improve her cooking without criticizing her. The sample bites she took made her mouth and heart pleased with the results. Her uncle and cousin also appreciated the fluffier biscuits added to their plates instead of the usual heavier variety.

The two men stopped at the bottom of the outside

stairs while she descended. Will tipped his hat.

"Good morning, Miss Kolek. Forgive our unannounced intrusion last night."

"Not at all, Mr. Johnson. We are happy to have you and your mother here."

"Mina, I plan on having Will stay with me at the hotel. Would it be asking too much hospitality for my ma to stay with you?" Jack said.

Her gaze lifted to accommodate his taller stature.

"I can guarantee Daniel and Uncle Silas will have no objections, and I will love her company. She might get a little rest while we are at work tomorrow."

Will's serious face gave up a smile. "Thank you, ma'am. We only plan to stay a few days." He nodded and trudged up the stairs.

Jack walked over to the hitching post and propped both hands there while looking across the street. Mina's nose twitched at the smell of soap, and her eyes widened, taking in his dress clothes.

"Jack, you look like a real city gentleman. Are you planning on church this morning?"

He released one hand to rub his bare face. She felt her face grow warm. Oh, my—his now visible and very handsome face and those green eyes—offset by long, chestnut hair hanging under his hat—took her breath. She thought about all the years she had wondered about the color of Jack Johnson's eyes. She sighed.

"Now I need a haircut," he said.

"I suppose so," Mina said.

Jack removed his derby and twirled it on one finger before grasping it with both hands and stepping toward her. "Mina—"

They both startled at the sound of the door opening.

Silas, Will, and Mrs. Johnson made their way down the stairs.

Uncle Silas spoke as they descended. "Good morning, Jack. Are you ready, Mina?"

"Yes, sir. It appears the pastor will have more people in his congregation today," she said.

A weary looking Daniel waited for them in his buggy with Miss O'Connor beside him. Mina noticed the extra horses tied to the hitching rail beside the buggy. Her cousin yawned.

"I rented these two horses for Jack and Will for this morning. My buggy will only hold three more," Daniel said.

"We can walk," Jack said.

"And come in late for the sermon? I think not."

Mina touched her uncle's arm when her cousin yawned again. He cleared his throat.

"Daniel, let me take the reins. Your night spent delivering a baby has tired you a mite."

Her cousin hesitated but nodded. "Yes, a breech delivery. I almost lost both of them, but Miss O'Connor's experience at the Women's hospital in Boston helped her assist me."

His fiancée gave him a grateful smile.

Daniel turned to their uncle. "Silas, do you know if Mrs. Cosgrove might need more help in the store within the next few months? The young mother is in need of employment."

"Business has picked up with all the new people moving to Denver. I'll ask her after church," Silas said.

"Is the mother the lady who is staying with the Methodist preacher and his wife? Mrs. Davis?" Mina asked.

"Yes, her husband became ill during their trip here and died. She suspects food poisoning, but, in viewing the body, I think he suffered from ruptured intestines."

"How sad for them," Mrs. Johnson said. "What did she name the baby?"

"Beulah Maureen Davis," Miss O'Connor said.

Mina's mouth dropped open. "That is unusual. Did she get it from the land described in the Bible by that name?"

Daniel smiled. "It's interesting. Yes, in a way. You see, they heard a new hymn at a church service in Philadelphia last year by a Mr. Stites mentioning that land. They thought it so lovely and decided to use Beulah if they had a girl."

"It *is* lovely," Mrs. Johnson said.

"Yes, and so is that precious baby," Shannon said.

Mina noticed Will and Jack exchanged a look. Their mother watched them with a gentle smile. Her long buried grief for her own mother stirred.

She pushed away the deep ache once they arrived at church and tried to focus on the songs, prayers, and sermon once she squeezed herself between Jack and her Uncle Silas on the pew.

Mrs. Cosgrove approached them after church to ask them to lunch.

"After Mrs. Johnson and her son stopped by the store looking for you yesterday morning, I knew Dr. Cummings would not be prepared for Sunday lunch today. I didn't know you and Mina would return with Jack last night, but I've made plenty."

Mina realized the close ages of Mrs. Cosgrove and Mrs. Johnson. She thought back to when she first met the Cosgroves. The couple who cared for her while

Silas was away could not have children. They'd loved her like a daughter.

Mrs. Johnson opted to ride with Mrs. Cosgrove. Once at the widow's home, they chatted and worked to ready the table like old friends. Both widowed women visibly relaxed in each other's company; the empathy of shared circumstances removed any haughty social female airs. Mina thought of the women in Chicago who cared more about impressing others with their calling cards and social status, but not these two women. Mina realized how much you miss about people until something happens to show you the overlooked layers.

As the full plates became empty, Jack stood.

"Mrs. Cosgrove, this was delicious. I may have an unusual request. I'd like you to accompany my mother into your sitting room to visit while I do the dishes."

Everyone at the table laughed, but his mother smiled.

"Thank you, Jack."

"I'd like to make sure he doesn't break anything. I'm helping," Mina said.

Daniel rose, turning to their hostess. "Thank you for a delicious dinner, Mrs. Cosgrove. Also, I appreciate your willingness to consider hiring Mrs. Davis."

"You are very welcome, Dr. Cummings. Silas and I might benefit from additional help at the store. Mina keeps her focus on my ledgers where I want it. When we get busy, I hate pulling her away from the books to help with the customers. Mrs. Davis might be who we need. Tell her to come see me when she's ready."

"Indeed I will. Now, we really should take our leave. Thank you again." Daniel moved to assist his nurse with her chair.

Miss O'Connor tried to hide a yawn and stood.

Uncle Silas chuckled and grinned. "I'm going to see Miss O'Connor and my nephew home. Once we see her safely tucked into her room behind the office, we will wait for everyone upstairs. I'm feeling a mite tired myself." He straightened his left arm like it hurt. "Yep, these old bones are a bit achy today."

Will also stood. He migrated towards the door like the others. "I'll take the horses back to the livery to avoid more fees. If it's all right, I'll come by and get your buggy before I return to pick up everyone still here, Mr. Kolek."

"That's fine, Will." Her uncle turned and gave their hostess a slight bow with an air of mock formality laced with genuine sentiments. "Thank you for a fine meal and your remarkable hospitality, Miriam Cosgrove."

Their hostess laughed and smiled. She gave his bearded face a fond pat. "You're very welcome, Silas." She saw her old friend to the door along with the others. Then she returned to where Mrs. Johnson waited. "Well, Emily, I feel plain spoiled. Shall we have a chat?"

"Yes, Miriam, let's do," Emily Johnson said.

Mina and Jack gathered the plates and took them to the kitchen, placing them on the table beside the pump and basin.

She hurried to place the kettle on Mrs. Cosgrove's cast iron stove to heat the water to wash the dishes. When she turned from the stove, Jack stood by the doorway leading from the kitchen to the dining room. He placed a hand on her arm and held a finger to his lips. She took a step to pass him. "I need to check—"

Jack shook his head. The voices of his mother and Mrs. Cosgrove carried from the close alcove of the parlor.

She missed the first of the conversation but the next words explained Jack's demeanor.

"No, I didn't get a chance to visit with Jack alone after he came back home this time, nor have I talked to him without others present here. That's fine, but I do want to know how he fared during the years away." Emily Johnson laughed. "Not that he'd tell me the way he used to as a boy. He's long past that. I guess my main hope is to find he's not learned so much in his schooling and travels as to find me obsolete. Our neighbor's daughter came home from school in the east with a new husband and her poor mother realized her daughter no longer found her opinions of merit. Her own offspring told her the way she'd raised her and cared for her were outdated. She knew more of science, health, and business than her parents imagined. My Lee and I found it sad. Her parents did the best they could; a right fine job in my opinion. Her mother kept that girl alive during the war years."

Mrs. Cosgrove's voice reached them. "I understand a bit. My husband and I never had children but helped Silas with Mina, so when she returned from school with all these ideas regarding efficiency for the store and bookkeeping, it pricked my pride a bit. However, I must give her credit for presenting it in such a way as not to dismiss our way of doing things. She showed me *how* the new ways helped. Mina's outspoken ways sometimes give people the wrong impression of her. I found she spoke her mind, waiting for consideration or rejection outright from the time of her youth. Growing up as a young orphan in the isolation of the mountains most of her life made her think about things too long. She belabors a single idea and ponders it until her nails are gnawed to nubs."

Guilt for eavesdropping turned Mina's stomach. She met Jack's gaze, which mirrored her emotions. He turned and crossed to the basin.

Jack removed his suit coat and rolled up his sleeves. Mina brought the hot water from the stove. He took it from her and poured it in the basin.

"I'll start on these plates while you finish clearing the table," Jack said.

Mina hurried to the dining room to retrieve the glasses and utensils. Mrs. Johnson and Mrs. Cosgrove continued to talk as she hurried her task to avoid notice and returned to the kitchen.

"We had no right to listen to them. Let's not discuss it. I'll wash and you dry," she said as Jack placed the plates in the water.

"Let me spare your delicate hands," Jack said.

She laughed, but he didn't move away. "Truly, Jack?"

"In truth, I guess I'd have to inspect to see for sure," he said.

Mina held her breath as he took both of her hands in his and ran a finger from where her quickening pulse beat at her wrists, across each palm to the length of her fingers. He turned them over and caressed the backs with his thumbs.

"Hmmm—" He lifted her right hand. "This one is mighty delicate except for this one rough spot here."

She trembled as he kissed a spot on one knuckle. Before she recovered, he lifted her left hand.

"And this one is very soft except for this spot." He kissed the center of the back of it.

His green eyes sparkled with humor, turning to something else. The intensity of his gaze caused her heart to race more. Her mouth went dry.

"How dare—uh—I think I'll dry." She pulled back her hands and reached for the towel.

He stepped toward the basin and reached for the first plate.

They worked in silence for a while. She heated more water to rinse the dishes and brought it to the basin. He helped her stack the clean dishes and glasses before they started on the utensils.

"Do you remember the man I talked with at the court house in Hot Springs?" he asked.

She took a deep breath. How could he have a new offer? "I thought you said the letter I brought you only listed general city work projects. You didn't mention an offer."

"That's right, it didn't. Anyway, he sent another letter with Will. They have a situation for me with the county," Jack said.

She dried the fork he handed her. "What about the railroad extension work in Colorado?"

He handed her the last of the utensils from the now empty basin. After drying his hands, he threw the towel over his shoulder and crossed his arms over his chest, leaning against the sideboard.

"That offer still exists, as well as a couple more. What do you think?"

Before she answered, his mother, who'd entered the kitchen as he spoke, did.

"I never thought I'd hear you ask for someone's

opinion, son."

Jack ducked his head with a sheepish grin. He lifted his eyes and looked from his mother to Mina. "Actually, I wouldn't mind both of your opinions. It's in regard to the work in Hot Springs or here."

Mrs. Johnson walked over to the clean dishes stacked and placed on the small table. She picked up a glass for closer inspection before returning it to its spot. "You did a fine job getting these ready for use at the next meal. They are clean and prepared to serve their intended purpose. Miriam owns them, so she gets to decide where and when she uses them. You are God's child Jack and His providence has caused you to travel a path to attain the work skills you have. Those skills are the same wherever you use them. What's important is taking into account the people He's also put in your life—to complete it. Will and I came to see you. Now you know that your family's arms are open for your return to Arkansas, but only God can tell your heart if being there is more important than being here."

Mina held her breath. Maybe, she should excuse herself so Jack's mother could talk to him, but she did not want to interrupt his mother. So she watched Mrs. Johnson take the towel off her son's shoulder, fold it, and hand it back. She watched Jack's face as his mother continued.

"The Bible has many stories about the dangers of looking back. We can't go back to the places and people of the past. If the Lord chooses to put some of those same places and people in our present or future, we must look forward to the new purposes he has for those in our lives. It has to be a longing for what the Lord is doing now, not for clinging to what's already been. There's a big difference. It's fine to cherish our memories, just don't let them keep you from walking forward. Selfishly, I'd like all my children close, but I'll be just as proud if God continues to use you to reach places and people for His purpose here. I've said my piece and will send Miriam in to direct you to where these things go in her cupboard."

Jack never spoke; his face reflected respect and tenderness as his mother left the room.

The drip from the pump sounded amplified in the silence.

"Jack—" Mina started. She rubbed the backs of her hands, where the memory of the warmth of his lips remained. Her pulse quickened. "Why *do* you care what *I* think, Jack?"

Miriam Cosgrove bustled into the room clasping her hands in delight.

"My, my, everything is gleaming. Thank you both, dears. I'll put them away quicker on my own. I thank you but am shooing you home. Will is here to collect you."

She kissed Mina on the cheek and patted Jack's arm. "I know Mr. Johnson will want to see you home before returning to the hotel."

~

Mina pointed out places of interest to Mrs. Johnson and related the history of the town on the way home. They continued to talk as they approached in the buggy until Miss O'Connor ran down the stairs in obvious distress.

Mina jumped down without waiting for assistance.

Shannon O'Connor met her, tears streaming down her face. "Mina, Mina—"

"What is it, Shannon?"

"It's your uncle. He—"

Mina's head reeled. She refused to hear any more. Her whole childhood swirled like a kaleidoscope of images as she dashed around Shannon and up the stairs.

Daniel knelt by their uncle on the floor. A pillow cradled his silver-haired head. Her cousin removed his stethoscope and shook his head upon seeing her.

"No!" she screamed, sinking to her knees and laying her head on his chest. No sound. She pressed her cheek against his still warm face. No breath welcomed or reassured her. She dissolved against the encapsulation of uncle-father-mother held within this one man–her only present family since the age of five-years

Will, Jack, and Mrs. Johnson arrived; they stood silent as Daniel sank back on his heels and finally sat with his now useless healing hands on his knees. Shannon sank down behind him.

"He went up here while I settled Miss O' Connor and replenished my medical bag for tomorrow. I heard a loud thud and dashed up here to find him on the floor. It was his heart, a massive cardiac arrest. I couldn't revive him, Mina."

She heard his words in a numbing haze of denial and harsh reality. Paralysis of her very being seemed to linger for a few more minutes before she lifted her head and acknowledged the others.

"Please leave me alone with him for a bit. We were alone for many years." Her voice broke. "Please go get Mrs. Cosgrove and our pastor." Tears streamed.

"Mina, let us move him," Daniel said.

She removed the pillow and slid his head onto her

lap. "No, leave us."

Once the door shut, tears flowed unhindered down her face. She went through a collage of memories with the only other person who shared them:

"Uncle Silas, do you remember when we . . . ?"

She talked to him until her spent voice became hoarse. The last shared vestige of life trailed off in a whisper.

The door opened and the soft arms of Mrs. Cosgrove encircled her from behind.

"He's gone, Mrs. Cosgrove. He's gone," she whispered.

Gratitude filled her as the familiar arms held her, as in the past—when she allowed it.

"Mina, you've always pushed to be stronger than your years required. Now, let us bolster your strength. God has sent family and friends for this time."

"No, they don't understand."

Mrs. Cosgrove hugged her closer and whispered. "No grief is exact. But the Johnsons have known grief and their most recent is still coming in ebbing waves. Your cousin has lost an uncle he's come to love and respect. Don't throw the solace God sends away."

No words passed her lips; her voice too spent to fight.

"Mina, you must let your cousin and the undertaker have him now. Our pastor is here."

She allowed the dear woman to help her ease Uncle Silas back onto the pillow once more. Mina bent and kissed his dear bearded cheek one last time. She then allowed them to lead her to a chair at the table.

Mrs. Cosgrove opened the door to their pastor, accompanied by Bevil Henry and her friend Betsy.

"Pastor, please go with him. Don't let him be alone," Mina said.

"Mina, my dear, he's not alone," their pastor said. "He's gone home. But Mrs. Cosgrove and I will go with his earthly vessel to see everything is well tended. Pastor Henry and Miss Singer will stay with you."

"Thank you," Mina said.

Betsy scooted her chair next to hers and took her hand without saying a word. Mina squeezed her friend's hand, grateful for her friendship and understanding.

Bevil Henry bowed his head. "Dear Lord, Miss Kolek is grieving. You understand grief. I pray comfort for her—Your comfort—no one here can give that to her. Guide us to see her needs, and I pray You will use us as Your hands and feet to meet those. Thank You for Your servant Silas Kolek. I only knew him a short time but for those who loved him during his journey on this earth, please send joy in remembering him. In Jesus's name, Amen."

She sighed. *How perfect.* Her swollen eyes met his as he lifted his head. "Thank you."

Daniel and the undertaker entered with two other men and placed her uncle in blankets. Mrs. Cosgrove and their family minister left with them.

The swish and brush of a passing dress stirred Mina's notice. Mrs. Johnson headed to the back rooms, but she returned a few minutes later and approached her with a look of compassionate determination.

"Miss Kolek, you must allow Miss Singer and me to help you get ready for bed. I've turned your covers down, and your gown is ready. You must sleep. Tomorrow will be a busy and draining day."

Mina nodded.

They led her to her room, and for the first time in her life, she allowed others to tend her. Even at five, she'd asserted her independence to her uncle. The tidal wave of the often forgotten grief from the loss of her parents at such a young age returned and merged with the new wave from the loss of her uncle. She collapsed on the bed after they fastened the last button on her gown.

Although the light outside the window reflected early evening, weariness settled. Mrs. Johnson tucked the heavy covers around her.

"I'll be back in the morning," Betsy said after putting away Mina's clothes.

"Thank you, Bets."

Mrs. Johnson smoothed the covers once more. "Try to rest, my dear."

She nodded, but when Emily Johnson joined Betsy at the door, she stopped her.

"Mrs. Johnson, where's Jack?"

A moment of hesitation passed before the answer came.

"He's been waiting right outside the front door."

"Please don't find this inappropriate, but I'd like him to sit with me until I go to sleep," Mina said. She licked her dry, swollen lips, and tried to sniff and breathe out of her stuffy nose. Anguish and certainty squeezed her heart.

An understanding smile lifted Mrs. Johnson's lips. "I've raised an honorable son."

The stillness in the now dark room suffocated her after the two women left, drawing her back to her childhood bed after her parents' deaths. She'd lain in the darkness then too, but no one came to sit with her. Instead, she'd only heard the voices outside her room discussing sending her to Colorado. Each of her relatives gave reasons to disallow her residence with them. A long-standing resentment resulted until she came to stay with the Cummings during college. Getting to know her aunt brought insight into the circumstances a child never sees. Still, at the time, she feared the journey and the unknown uncle. She'd chewed her fingernails all the way to Denver. Then she met Silas Kolek. The uncle her aunt told her went to college, but decided to leave home for the west due to a family issue. None of it made sense to her young mind.

A poignant smile appeared at the memory of their introduction. The strong and still fit fifty-something-year old man squatted in front of her and stuck out his hand. He didn't force her to love him. She remembered his kind eyes when he asked to tuck her in that first night and his smile when she refused him. The nightmares waking her during her first week after they made the journey to the cabin changed her. Uncle Silas rushed to her in the darkness, not even stopping to light a lantern. She threw her small arms around him and felt safe for the first time since losing her parents. That feeling remained until her adolescent years when he traveled without her for work. Still, she learned to count on the Cosgroves, knowing her uncle did the work for her future.

The squeak of the door drew her gaze. Jack pushed the door, leaving it ajar behind him.

"Please sit with me again," she said.

He nodded, but ignored the chair beside her bed. Instead, he slid to the floor next to the bed once again.

She let her hand fall off the bed and onto his shoulder; he reached up and took it.

"Rest, Mina, I'm here."

She sighed. "Thank you, Jack."

Silent tears streamed down her cheeks, even as her aching heart prayed. The comfort of Jack's warm hand around hers suspended the tears. Sleep came.

A vague sense of the loss of that warmth settled a short time later, accompanied by whispered voices.

"You and Will go on to the hotel, Jack. I'll take Mr. Kolek's room tonight. That way Mina can rest, and I'll get up and take care of everything here without disturbing her," Mrs. Johnson said.

"Are you sure, Ma? I know this must be hard for you. You're not past losing Pa; too much grief compounded. I can stay," Jack said.

A pronounced silence followed.

His ma's voice vacillated between a whisper and a soft voice choked with emotion. "I'm sure, Jack. Losing your pa is nothing to get past. For me, his absence is truly missing the other half of myself. But the good Lord will give me grace and fill that void for me to continue. Are you past losing your pa?"

More silence.

"No, ma'am. There's just no helping it."

"Let's just help Mina now. We'll talk more later, Jack. Losing Silas is more devastating than we can understand."

Mina frowned and turned her head. Uncle Silas— the curtain of sleep reclaimed her.

~

The number of people at the funeral and graveside overwhelmed her at the end of the week. It attested to

Silas Kolek's quiet but steady parameter of influence from years within the territory.

Regardless of the cold weather, people came, even Mr. Mathias. Of course, the imposed escort to the door, after the church service, enforced the request for only close friends and family to follow to the graveside.

The outpouring of food started on Monday.

Now, the week after the funeral, sitting in the attorney's office shook her. She didn't understand. Her uncle never acquired much in the way of material possessions. Another surprise came with those receiving a request to attend. Besides herself and her cousin, Mrs. Cosgrove, Jack Johnson, Old Toby, and their pastor came when summoned.

The attorney, Mr. Simmons, adjusted his wire-framed spectacles over his ears and pushed them up on his nose. He eyed the small group over the frame's rims for a moment before picking up the paper on his desk.

"Silas Kolek was a solid man. I met him when I first came to the territory a couple of years ago. My only regret is not meeting him at a younger stage in life. I would have treasured his friendship even more. Anyway, please allow me to express my deepest condolences to each of you, especially to you Miss Kolek. I'm afraid the things in this document will surprise you more than anyone here, other than Mr. Johnson." He turned an assessing stare on Jack. "Sir, you made an indelible impression on Mr. Kolek. The items pertaining to you were present in the original document we prepared. He's only added a few items this past month and brought this poem by last week. I'll read it after presenting the items in his last will and testament. So, I'll begin."

He first read all the standard legal jargon present about being in sound body and mind at the start. Then the list of bequeathed items started. Mrs. Cosgrove received his half of the store ownership. The mountain claim and cabin went to Old Toby. The donation of all of his clothes—except for his favorite hat and jacket, which he left to Mina—to the church and those in need came as no surprise. Daniel received his wagon, buggy, horse, and furniture. The lawyer paused in his recitation.

Mina sat in stunned silence. She wanted the cabin, but knew Toby needed it for now. Maybe—she'd think about it later.

Mr. Simmons cleared his throat. "Now, to the matter of the money he held in the bank, and this may be more than you realized. The original provision stands for its equal division between Miss Kolek and Mr. Jack Johnson. He allocated part of his money while Miss Kolek attended school. He'd worked hard to save money for your schooling and did not have much left at that time. However, he did some profitable and diverse mining ventures with old friends, including Mr. Toby McEntire here, and struck enough. Anyway, the amount is $15,000 plus the amount in his account for daily items, at present totaling $900, with $100 of that to go to the church. Those figures are all after my fee, paying out of his obligations for items owed and the funeral."

Mina glanced at Jack's shocked face.

"Why?" he asked Mr. Simmons.

The lawyer leaned forward. "I don't know. Until last week, the stipulation of the need to find you returned to Rockport, reconciled with your family, and building a good life in Rockport, Arkansas—per his original advice to you—existed. However, he amended that last week. After meeting you again, his regard increased. To be honest, I think he rather hoped—well, his niece has always known her own mind; anyway, he also left this poem for both of you. I haven't read it, and it's sealed at his request. All I know is he started it after meeting Mr. Johnson and only finished it last week."

Mina felt numb. He'd raised her; made sure she went to college and left her enough to start her own life. Still—she didn't understand. The issue of women owning property seemed archaic to her, as many now did, including Mrs. Cosgrove, but still, she knew current society's limitations for young women in her current position. None of it mattered right now. She nodded at Mr. Simmons.

"Is that it?"

Mr. Simmons opened his right desk drawer, pulled out two envelopes, and slid them toward her. "No, ma'am. In one of these is the poem, and a deed and a letter to you are in the other one."

She reached for the one marked "Deed" first. He pulled it back and slid the other envelope toward her.

"I suggest you, your cousin, and Mr. Johnson read this first. Even though I don't know the words he used, the deed reveals his heart to me. He realized the territory where he raised you would change once it became a state. Denver is going to continue to grow. He wanted something different for you." Mr. Simmons stood. "Now, if the pastor, Mrs. Cosgrove, and Toby will walk with me to the other room, we can sign all the necessary papers for their portions. That is, if it is acceptable to Dr. Cummings, and he can sign later." He smiled at Daniel's perplexed expression. "Please, excuse me, Dr. Cummings; I failed to mention that Silas named you as the final executor of his wishes. Are you in agreement, sir? And do you wish to finalize it today?"

Daniel rubbed his brow for a moment. "Yes, yes, of course."

Mr. Simmons reached into his drawer once more and withdrew another envelope. He handed it to Daniel. "Your uncle left this letter for your mother, Dr. Cummings. It also holds your grandmother's locket. Will you see both reach her?"

Her cousin nodded and took the envelope.

After the group left, Mina reached for the envelope containing the poem. Her hands shook as she unfolded it, and her voice faltered and broke during her first attempt. Jack reached for the paper.

"May I?"

She nodded.

Tears coursed down her face as she listened.

Dearest Mina, Jack and Daniel,

Forgive my imperfect verse. I hope by the time you read this, your lives are settled beyond my hopes and dreams for each of you. If so, my words might only bring a shake of your heads at what I didn't know and your actual choices. However, if the Lord takes me sooner, maybe these words will give you pause and consideration. Mina, I'm sure you know, but I want to say the words. You are beyond my niece. In my heart, you became my daughter. I'll be sure to thank God and your parents for the privilege. Jack and Daniel, you're good men. Please see after our girl. Godspeed.

With My Greatest Affection,

Silas Kolek

Jack shuffled the top page under the next two. Mina reached for the handkerchief Daniel offered her. She nodded at Jack. "Please continue, Jack."

Jack cleared his throat and glanced at her and back to the page. "Here's his poem."

The blast killed all but two.
It left nothing for the old man or young one to do.
Nothing to do but wait.
To see if they'd see rescue or Heaven's gate.
They talked a bit to pass the time.
The old man even shared a nomad's regret in rhyme.
The young man showed familiar brashness, but a shade of family regret.
Many things left unresolved, the old man bet.
So, he gave him the advice that he wished someone had given him.
Their rescue came, and he knew the memory of his words might dim.
Still, he did not forget the young man through nary a season.
He spoke to his niece of this young man for some reason.
She too became curious about the young man's plight.
Did he go home or face a loner's fight?
They often included him in their prayers.
Hoping his life only held the best of cares.
Plans for a fanciful trip to visit the young man's family home, they tossed about—
Even though, the cost might prove stout.
The old man used his remaining strength to make a way for his niece to attend college

and meet family in Illinois.
The absence of family stole many joys.
She did well and his heart filled with pride.
God's faithfulness returned her to his side.
He held amazement at the Creator's ways and plans
For his nephew sought to come to Denver with his healing hands.
The friendship the cousins formed during her college stage
brought more family to him in his advanced age.
His niece proposed they travel to meet her cousin, detouring south for their planned trip.
However, his sudden illness almost caused a dream to rip.
Something unexplainable made him agree with her tenacity and dream-filled soul.
She'd go alone, whether with train or beast to cajole.
Her cousin met her at the depot near Rockport.
She'd been followed by an unsavory sort.
Once there, things unfurled in events unforeseen.
The young man's long delayed return coincided, resulting in a brotherly
conflict scene.
His niece's dreams of the young man dissolved.
The imaginary conclusion of his choices now solved.
Still, something remained.
Instead of diverging their paths, life merged them, no longer strained.
The uncle still hoped his dream for the two young people might come true.
A beautiful impossible wedding of lives and a

couple as only God can do.

But his niece dashed his hopes by declining the young man's proposal,

He understood as it came from the young man's attempt to be noble.

The old man smiled, and said a prayer, leaving it up to God.

Only He would determine where the feet of these two trod.

At the end, Jack stared down at the floor.

"Jack?"

His green eyes lifted, bright with moisture. "Why did he think so much of me? I can't keep the money. It should be yours."

"Jack, Uncle Silas had a sense about people. I think God gave him the ability to see something in *you*—mirroring himself and all his early hopes and dreams. My only request is that you honor him with your choices. Maybe God's showing you it's time to go home. That's what I think."

Daniel nodded. "Jack, my cousin's words hold merit. However, Mina, the choice is still Jack's." He glanced at the other envelope. "Are you going to open it?"

Mina nodded and Jack handed it to her. A letter lay within the folds of the formal deed she removed from the envelope. Her hands shook and tears flowed as she read the first two paragraphs to herself. She stopped. Daniel and Jack needed to hear this. She started over, this time reading aloud.

My dearest Mina,

You've been the biggest blessing in my life. I have

never ceased to thank God for sending you to me. Although, I must admit to holding many doubts when you first came. How did a drifter and bachelor approach raising a little girl? But God gave you the feistiness and tenacity to teach me. I love you, Mina. You've become a fine young woman. Very much like your mother.

I've never told you this, but the reason I left home has to do with your mother's sister, Anna. Your aunt captured my heart. She became ill and died while I attended college. I had one year left when she died. I never finished. Your mother and her parents blamed me. They said if I had married her and taken her with me—well, no one knows. The odd part is my family agreed with them. At the time, she seemed too young and I wanted to give her time while I went to school. My accomplishments and dreams disappeared. I headed west and never looked back or made contact.

That's part of the reason meeting Jack Johnson shook me. Maybe if I guided him back home, I'd redeem my choices. I laugh now, because God has used our meeting for such a bigger purpose. I started writing my sister then, and we forgave each other, and many other things.

If you're reading this, I have passed. It is my hope you will live in a small town in a community of people who treasure family. I love the adventurous souls who built this territory and shaped it into a state, but I know the rapid influx of people will be a flood for a while of ne'er-do-wells, unscrupulous businessmen, amid the handful of solid families. A town with deeper roots is my hope for you.

You will find the deed for land in Rockport,

Arkansas enclosed here.

Jack's head shot up and he scooted to the edge of his chair.

She licked her dry lips and continued.

Please forgive me for not telling you a few things. I have never been dishonest with you—just withheld a few things. You see, after meeting Jack Johnson years ago, I did more than wonder about him. After recovering from my injuries and writing you about my next job, I took a detour to Rockport. Of course, Jack was not there, but his family was. I met his parents, his brother Will and Will's fiancée, Alice Cushman. At that time, they also held hopes of his returning home and told me about him. His parents demonstrated great kindness and thanked me for taking an interest in their son. I told them about you. Mina, you were fifteen at the time if you remember. The area impressed me. I asked if they would notify me if a piece of land close to theirs ever became available. We wrote about once a year. It became clear that Jack would not return home soon, but I never gave up hope. His continuing his schooling encouraged me. That's why I still wanted us to plan our trip, even though my desire to move there did not happen. However, a couple of years ago, his father wrote to me. He'd fallen and his health impacted his farm's production. His finances suffered. He didn't want Jack or his eldest son, Marc, to feel obligated to come home. His middle son, Will, did not agree. Mr. Johnson sold me twenty-five acres of his land. This is the deed you now hold in your hand. You have a choice—you can keep it and build a home on it or you can sell it to Will Johnson, if he is now able, or to Jack Johnson. You decide.

If you sell it and decide to stay in Colorado, I'd prefer you move to a smaller area. Of course, I've designated Daniel as the overseer of this land trust for you. Have faith in my decisions.

Your cousin Daniel is able to handle Denver better than you can on your own. I know you won't stay with him forever, especially after he marries. There are too many men like George Mathias in the shadows, as well as in the light. You're smart, dear one, but this world is dangerous. The Good Lord will keep you safe, but He expects us to use common sense and to recognize our limitations. Now, stop your frowning at me, little one. Unscrupulous men can hurt men, as well as women. Surround yourself with friends of good character.

Mina, your old uncle never married, so please forgive my unrealistic dreams for you and Jack.

I wish you both well. My love is always with you.

Your Uncle,

Silas Kolek

Daniel stood, kissed her head, shook Jack's hand, and left, shutting the door behind him.

Jack vacated his chair and started pacing. After a few minutes, irritation set in and she stood.

"Jack Johnson, stop that. I'm as taken aback as you are. My uncle has surprised even me."

He stopped. "That old man never stopped pushing me toward home. If that don't— I can't—you can't."

Mina placed herself in front of him with her hands on her hips. "I said to stop." She stepped back and stumbled as he stepped closer. "Please."

He caught and steadied her. The look in his green eyes made her squirm. He bent his head, holding her blue gaze, his lips inches from hers. His warm breath moistened her lips, but he stepped away short of kissing her.

She shivered and swallowed while he turned away, rubbing the back of his neck with his hand. He then started for the door.

"I've changed my mind," she said.

He stopped and turned. "About?"

Emotions churned, and words abandoned her.

"Mina, there is too much to consider. I'm going back to the hotel and will stop by later to talk."

"Please, don't go," she said, finding her voice again. "I've changed my mind about you, about my answer—I mean—I will marry you."

His posture became rigid and his face inscrutable. "But you turned me down. What makes you think I held my offer for you?"

It took everything in her, but Mina knew with absolute certainty what to do. She crossed to where he stood, reached up on her tiptoes and kissed him. His arms slid around her, lifting and pulling her close. His lips caressed hers, and she surrendered her long-held heart.

Chapter Sixteen

Jack broke the kiss, and lifted both of her hands to his lips. She'd kissed *him*. He searched the depths of her sparkling blue eyes. "There's a compass of stars in your eyes, Mina. God gave me *you* to find my way home. I love you." She blinked, looking at him in a way no other woman ever had before.

"I love you too, Jack."

He shut his eyes, fighting the urge to gather her close again. Hearing those words did something inexplicable to him. A sense of urgency filled him.

"Let's go get Bevil," he said, offering his arm.

"Bevil? Why?" she asked, ignoring his courteous gesture of escort.

"I want him to marry us."

"Not *today*, Jack," she said. "There's too much to decide. I need to talk to Mrs. Cosgrove about the store. Maybe she can hire that young widow Daniel told us about—Mrs. Davis. We need to plan. I mean—do you want to live here or in Rockport or Hot Springs? You haven't even gotten to spend time with you mother like I wanted."

Her happiness in this mattered most to him. He took her hands in his. "Mina, I've talked a bit with my ma. She's not wanting to discuss my father's death with me. Her feelings are private and I have to honor that, but I do plan to give her any help she needs and have further discussions with Will about helping the family. Let's go."

He grabbed her hand and started for the door. She stumbled behind him and laughed.

"Slow down!"

Jack turned and she bumped into him. They both started laughing.

He squatted down and cupped her face in his hands. "Forgive me. I'll try to slow down." She gave him a gentle smile and he hugged her. "It's been an emotional day and part of me is afraid you'll change your mind. What do *you* want and where do *you* want to live, Mina?"

Her face held certainty. She reached up and stroked his face. "Jack, I won't change my mind. You've had my heart for a long time. I thought I'd lost my chance with you beyond friendship. Uncle Silas just gave me the nudge I needed to admit it. I love the mountains, but I'm going to trust Uncle Silas. Let's build a house in Rockport or Malvern, wherever the current city boundaries frame my property. He attached receipts of the yearly taxes he's paid to keep it. This way, we can both be there for your mother." Earnest yearning showed on her face.

Jack understood. Unlike many young women, Mina would welcome the thought of having her mother-in-law close by; she'd done without a mother most of her life. He could not stop himself from lifting her chin and bending his knees to put them at eye level. "She'll welcome you as a daughter."

She moved his hand from her chin and pressed his palm to her cheek. "Thank you, Jack."

So many emotions churned inside him. He cleared his throat and straightened, stepping away to calm his pounding heart. "I'm sure living in Hot Springs or Rockport won't impact my work offer. I'll have to travel during the days anyway." She frowned and Jack thought about her childhood experiences; in particular, the loss of her parents, and how the time when Silas traveled for work had created insecurities for her. His voice softened. "Mina, I will be home every night. If God is taking us there, the situation will work."

Jack reached for her hand, stroking the back of it with his thumb. She shivered and he smiled, stepping closer, but she placed a hand on his chest.

"I can't think straight if you kiss me again."

He grinned and bent his head. "Good. I don't want to think right now."

The sparkle in her eyes guided his heart. Jack kissed her with the love he'd tried to deny. She trembled against him as their lips parted. He gathered her into a hug, resting his cheek on top of her head.

Mina lifted her face and blushed, stepping away and smoothing her dress. "Daniel will come for me any moment. Let's . . . let's decide what we want before we tell Will and your mother. Of course, we'll need their input on a few things."

Jack did not care about decisions or telling anyone. He stepped toward her, but she fell back another step.

"Jack, *please*."

He made a face as he stepped forward and took both of her hands in his. She smiled and squeezed his hands.

"If we go back to Rockport with them, where will we stay until we can build a house?"

Jack laughed. She had no point of reference. "You haven't grown up where I did. My family and friends will make sure we have a place to stay."

"I have an idea." Mina's eyes twinkled. "I think we need to get Bevil and Betsy to go with us. We can get married in Rockport. I have a feeling about those two."

"Really? I guess women take more notice of those things."

Mina gave him an impish grin. "So, do you think they'd go?"

He scratched his head. "Why don't we concentrate on us for now, Mina? Bevil will refuse to marry us if I start putting a ring around his finger too." He took her hand and got down on one knee in front of her. "I know you changed your answer and have accepted my first proposal, but I want to ask again. Mina Jean Kolek will you do me the honor of taking my hand in matrimony?"

She laughed, but her eyes filled with tears. "I dreamed of you from the time Uncle Silas told me about the brash young man in the tunnel. You became a man I created. The reality of *you* took me aback—the reality of the man not the boy. The real Jack Johnson overwhelmed and frustrated me." Tears trickled down her cheeks even as she smiled down at him. "Then I got to know you. It took me bit to admit it, but I liked you"—she caressed his cheek—"and could count on you. I fell in love with you without trying. So, yes, Jack, I will give you my hand for the rest of our lives."

A lump formed in his throat as he gazed up at her, continuing to hold her hand. Overwhelming emotions made words impossible. The ones he managed to choke out after a time sounded inadequate to his ears, but they came from his heart as he gazed up at her. "Mina, your uncle mentioned his fifteen-year-old niece in the tunnel that day. Of course, that's enough to stir any young man's curiosity, but, at the time, my selfishness consumed me more than the thought of any girl. I didn't realize how much of my life I owed to your uncle until my older brother commented on it when I came home. It's a shame we didn't meet earlier. Anyway, I'm not one to look back much. My resentment of Will and Alice passed a long time ago for me. The reason for not going home after I started working for the railroad became the adventures and the work. I won't lie. This country boy enjoyed his travels. Still, my life started feeling pretty empty. God has a way of showing us the void present in the things of the world." He stood to his feet. "Mina, God used Silas to bring us together. I have no doubt. He picked you for me long before Silas did. I'm grateful." He offered her his arm. "Have we given this rational thought for long enough? May we go now?"

She smiled and nodded.

The door opened. Mina pressed her hands to her flushed and wet cheeks, looking at him. He took her left hand and tucked it in the crook of his right arm, facing her cousin who stood there with a stern look on his face.

"Daniel, I have once again asked for your cousin's hand, and this time she has accepted. We want to ask your blessing."

Daniel's face remained impassive and Jack feared he'd miscalculated the doctor's approval. Then the man winked at Mina.

"You finally got the man you dreamed about, my dear cousin."

"No, I got more. I got the *real* Jack Johnson," Mina said.

Daniel smiled. "I must agree that's much better." He turned to her fiancé. "Well, Jack, I give you my blessing. Mr. Simmons filled me in on the land deed you're holding, Mina. As you are to have a husband, we will get all the documents finalized after the wedding. When is it?"

"I'd like it to be as soon as we, and Bevil Henry, can get the legalities addressed. My ma and Will are here. You, *your* lovely fiancée and Mrs. Cosgrove are here. Mina suggested Rockport, but I want her family to be present. Then," he swallowed, meeting her eyes, "we will go to Rockport." He lifted his eyes. "Dear Lord, thank you and please thank Silas for us."

Mina hugged his arm close and joined his prayer. "Yes, thank you, Lord."

~

Giddiness overcame Mina as Jack lifted her from the buggy, took her hand and rushed up the stairs with her. The passers-by in front of her cousin's office smiled when she laughed. Mrs. Johnson opened the door just as they reached the top step.

"For goodness sake, Jack, let the girl catch her breath!"

Mina gulped for air and giggled when Jack dropped her hand like a guilty schoolboy as his mother ushered them inside. "I'm fine, Mrs. Johnson. We have so much to tell you."

Will folded his newspaper and stood. "Well, if you want to know why we kept our prior acquaintance with your uncle a secret, it's because he wanted it that way. So, do you want me to buy the land back now?"

Her future brother-in-law's unexpected defensiveness tempered her joviality a bit. She nibbled at a fingernail and shook her head. "No—"

Jack touched her arm and stepped in front of her. "Will, you aren't very observant." He inclined his head toward his mother with a grin. "Is he, Ma?"

She watched the small smile on Mrs. Johnson's face widen.

"Really, Jack?"

"Yes, ma'am."

Mina's heart overflowed as the dear woman rushed to her, enveloping her in the warmest hug she could ever remember. Tears spurted to her eyes and she returned her hug. "Thank you, Mrs. Johnson, I—"

Her future mother-in-law leaned back to look her in the face, but kept her arms around her. "I want you to call me Ma. You're to be my new daughter."

Tears streamed down her cheeks until the confusion on Will's face made her laugh.

Jack gave him a brotherly punch in the arm. "She's agreed to marry me." He cleared his throat. "And I was going to ask you to stand up with me and also see how you felt about our joining you on the train back to Arkansas, but . . . I don't know . . . you've got a foul disposition today."

Will's frown disappeared behind the second best smile Mina had ever seen. He laughed at the teasing look Jack gave him. They slapped each other on the backs.

"Of course, I'd be honored," Will said. "And to the second, that's fine by me. I welcome you." He glanced at her. "Both of you."

Mrs. Johnson placed her arm around Mina, watching. The tension left the room and a long lost camaraderie surfaced between the two men. No words or comments came as they witnessed the brother's seal their reconciliation for good.

~

Two weeks later, Mina stood at the back of the church holding her cousin's arm as organ music filled the sanctuary. Daniel swallowed hard and gave her an encouraging smile. "You look beautiful in Mrs. Cosgrove's dress. It meant so much to her for you to wear it. Thanks for letting me stand in for Uncle Silas. If the Lord allows it, I know both he and your parents are looking down smiling."

She hugged his arm. "I'm so grateful for you, Daniel. I love you."

He cleared his throat. "And I you. Are you ready?"

Mina gave him a bright smile and nodded. The sight of Bevil by the altar, flanked by Betsy on one side and Jack and Will to the other, urged her forward. The other people who filled the church pews blurred once her eyes met Jack's. His loving gaze held hers as Daniel escorted her down the aisle, never shifting until their hands joined and they turned toward Bevil. He smiled and addressed their family and friends.

"Jack and Mina's journey leading to this day started long before they met. God used a catastrophic event to introduce Jack Johnson to Silas Kolek. He had a plan beyond those circumstances to bring these two to this day. I've witnessed the Good Lord's mighty hand in so many lives, including my own, transforming tragedy into hope and joy. So, today we aren't only celebrating a wedding, we are praising God for His purpose in all things concerning these two, as well as in each of our lives. He amazes me every day. Learn to live in joyful amazement beyond your circumstances. Let us pray."

Mina's tears started the moment Jack helped her to kneel beside him and they bowed their heads. He had asked her if she minded saying their vows on their knees. His humbleness before the Lord pricked her heart. Bevil's prayer moved in seamless transition to the traditional vows. Jack's eyes once again met and held hers as he made his pledge to her with tenderness and certainty intoned in every word. The residual traces of every protective emotional barricade she'd built through the years crumbled. Unwavering love and trust resounded as she repeated her vows. Her heart shouted so much more than the formal words conveyed but those words were for Jack alone and too private to be spoken in public.

Betsy straightened the small lace train of her dress as Jack assisted her to her feet. Bevil smiled at them. "I now pronounce you man and wife. Jack you may kiss your bride."

Mina's heart soared as her husband's lips met hers. *Her husband.*

Jack lifted his head but didn't step away, instead he continued to gaze down at her and took her hands and whispered.

"I love you, my beautiful bride. Even the majesty and fleeting wonder of a starry sky can't steal my breath away as you do. You've taken it for a lifetime."

Mina lifted her hand to his cheek and whispered back. "I'll make sure you find your breath in me every day of our lives, my darling. You are every adventure my heart could dare, and your love removes all fears. I trust you without question. I love you, Jack."

Bevil smiled at them before they turned to face the rows of smiling faces.

"I present Mr. and Mrs. Jack Johnson."

~

A few days later, they stood on the railway platform waiting until the last call to board the train with his ma and Will. Mrs. Cosgrove stood with Daniel and Shannon on the platform with them, all delaying their goodbyes until the last moment. Jack understood and decided to give them a few moments alone. He caressed his wife's hand.

"Mina, I need to be sure they've loaded your trunk. I'll be back."

Mina nodded and smiled at him. He lost his breath. His wife. The awkwardness and absolute perfection of the clumsy but loving completion of their first night washed over him. She surprised him in her determination to see it through. Her fierce love for him got her past the initial pain. Once resolved, the mystery of their subsequent loving unfolded and grew each time. They belonged to each other as one. He had never understood what that meant before.

An elbow caught his ribs, gaining his attention.

"I'll go with you," Will said.

Jack glanced to where his mother stood beside Mina.

"Hurry up you two. We don't want to board without you," she said.

His brother fell in step beside him. They hurried on their errand. The porter informed them all trunks and luggage were loaded. Will grinned at him.

"You knew they would be."

He shrugged. "I thought they would, but it never hurts to check, and besides, Mina needed some time to say goodbyes without me. She is leaving everything she's ever known for me. Even though she loves me, it's hard."

"Yep. I'm glad Alice and I have never had to face leaving loved ones behind for a life in another place. But we've faced people leaving too many times. I know how Daniel and Mrs. Cosgrove feel," Will said.

A residual ache of regret brought a frown to Jack's face.

Will slapped him on the shoulder. "We're past that brother. Let's head back. We need to board."

The sight of the man who stood across from Mina at the opposite end of the platform quickened Jack's steps. Will hurried to keep up with him.

"Jack, what—"

A man stepped in front of him. "Mr. Johnson, I understand you are leaving town today."

Jack clinched his jaw, glancing around the deputy who blocked his way. He noted Daniel had moved to stand beside Mina with the other women clustered around them. They faced the gambler addressing them. Jack tore his eyes away from the scene to meet the knowing eyes of the lawman. "Yes, sir. Do you realize who is speaking to my wife? I need you to remove Mr. Mathias or get out of my way and allow me to do what is needed."

The deputy rocked back on his heels. "Indeed I do.

My thought is to keep you from ending up in our jail instead of on the train. Let's just say I'm aware and will supervise this unfortunate encounter."

Will cleared his throat. "My brother is beyond conversation, sir. Does he have permission to make a more effective statement?"

The deputy turned. "Let's see. After you."

Jack reached Mina, and Daniel stepped back, for him to take his place beside her. He noted his wife's pale face. All thoughts of social amenities or reserve left him. He knocked the smirking man flat on the platform. He shook his fist and stepped back at the murmurs from others around them.

The deputy behind him turned and waved off the people starting toward them. "I have this situation handled, ladies and gentlemen. Go ahead and board."

Jack stepped back as the gambler shook his head and struggled to rise.

"Deputy, arrest this man. He assaulted me," Mr. Mathias said.

The deputy stepped around Jack and assisted Mr. Mathias to his feet. "That's not accurate. Mr. Johnson only enforced the decree for you to stay away from Miss Kolek—I mean Mrs. Johnson, his wife. It's you I'm arresting."

The gambler smirked. "I am free to come to the train station and have freight arriving."

"Of course you do, Mr. Mathias, but you chose to approach Mrs. Johnson, therefore, you are coming with me." The lawman nodded to the small group. "Have a good trip." He took Mr. Mathias by the elbow. "Let's go."

"All aboard," the conductor called to the waiting

passengers.

Jack turned to Daniel. He shook his new cousin-in-law's hand. "I'll take good care of her."

"See that you do. Shannon and I will plan a trip to see you within the year, after we marry," Daniel said.

Jack waited as Mina hugged Mrs. Cosgrove one last time. Shannon gave her a kiss on the cheek. His mother patted his shoulder and headed for the train with Will. Jack held his arm out and Mina took it.

Once boarded and in their seats across the aisle from Will and his mother, he caught Mina's gaze and kissed her hand. She stroked his bruising knuckles. "Thank you, my love."

Jack clenched and extended the sore fingers on his right hand a few times. The happiness and trust on Mina's face made it worth it. "You're my wife. I'll protect you with my life."

She leaned her head against his arm and sighed.

"Are you sure about leaving Denver?" he asked.

Mina lifted her head. She glanced out the window one last time before turning back to him. Her eyes glowed. "I'm glad Mrs. Cosgrove hired Mrs. Davis and Betsy to help her at the store. Everything is as it should be. Let's go home."

"I'm there," Jack said. He stroked her cheek with the back of his fingers.

Confusion passed over Mina's face.

"My brother Marc once told me he found his home in Florence, his wife. It didn't matter where they lived. I understand that now. Let's go to Rockport and build our new life together. We're already home."

""Yes," she said as she hugged his arm. "We're family, my love."

Jack kissed the top of his wife's head and smiled across the aisle at his mother and brother.

The train whistle sounded and the iron wheels vibrated on the rails, starting their new life.

THE END

AUTHOR'S NOTES
AND
RESOURCES FOR RESEARCH AND
FURTHER READING

Please Note: There are no quotes from any of the Research sources listed and websites are current as of the dates visited, so some may change or no longer be available. It is not an exhaustive list of all the research completed. I found these relevant and helpful for understanding and capturing this historic period for my fictional novel. The actual historical places, events, and the few actual historical people mentioned are utilized in a fictional sense, as a backdrop, and are indicated per my notes for this fictional story. The reader will find the following research resources helpful in learning more about the true history of the period—this novel and my characters are works of fiction.

Abbott, Dan, McCoy, Dell A., and McLeod, Robert W., 2007. *Colorado Central Railroad, Golden, Central City, Georgetown,* Sundance Books, Copyright 2007, Sundance Publications, Ltd., Denver, Colorado

Andrews, E. Benjamin, president of Brown University, 1895, 1896. *The History of the Last Quarter-Century in the United States 1870-1895, Volumes I and II,* New York, Charles Scribner's Sons, MDCCCXCVI, Copyright 1895, 1896, Press of J.J. Little & Co., Astor Place, New York

Anthony, Susan B., 1886. *History of Woman Suffrage, In Three Volumes., Volume*

III., 1876-1885, edited by Elizabeth Cady Stanton, Susan B. Anthony, and Matilda Joslyn Gage, Rochester, N.Y, A Public Domain Book. Accessed via eBook. *Author's Note: These three volumes will lend more information to the reader on the subject of the early woman's suffrage movement, and they include information about one of the movement leaders, Lucy Stone/ Lucy Stone Blackwell, mentioned by name only within this novel. My fictional character, Mina, admires her. However, there are some views expressed in these volumes not shared by the author.

Anthony, Susan B., Stanton, Elizabeth Cady and Gage, Matilda Joslyn, 1881. Anthony, Susan B., 1887, History of Woman Suffrage, In Three Volumes. Volume I. 1848-1861, edited by Elizabeth Cady Stanton, Susan B. Anthony and Matilda Joslyn Gage, Second Edition,1889, Susan B. Anthony, Rochester, N.Y., Charles Mann, London; Paris.

Anthony, Susan B., Stanton, Elizabeth Cady and Gage, Matilda Joslyn, 1881. History of Woman Suffrage, In Three Volumes. Volume II. 1861-1876, **edited by Elizabeth Cady Stanton, Susan B. Anthony and Matilda Joslyn Gage, Rochester, N.Y. A Public Domain Book. Accessed via eBook.**

Bailey, William Francis, *1906. The Story of the First Trans-Continental Railroad Its Projectors, Construction and History, A Public Domain Book,* **copyright 1906 by W. F. Bailey, Press of Pittsburg Printing Co.,**

accessed via eBook.

Collier, Captain Calvin L., U.S. Air Force, 1959, *They'll Do To Tie To! Hood's Arkansas Toothpicks, The Story of the Third Regiment, Arkansas Infantry C.S.A.,* **Third Printing July 1988, Civil War Round Table Associates by Eagle Press, Little Rock, Arkansas.**

Davis, Elmer O., 1948, *The First Five Years of the Railroad Era in Colorado: June 19, 1867, to June 19, 1872, Julesburg to Pueblo in Five Years,* **Compiled by E.O.** *Davis, 1948,* **Sage Books, Inc., Golden, Colorado.**

Digerness, David S. and the Editors of Sundance Books, 1978. *The Mineral Belt, Volume II-Old South Park- Across the Great Divide: An Illustrated History,* **Copyright 1978 by Sundance Publications Ltd., Silverton, Colorado.**

Fite, Gilbert C., University of Oklahoma, 1966, edited by Ray Allen Billington, *Histories of the American Frontier: The Farmers Frontier 1865-1900,* **Holt, Rinehart and Winston, Inc.**

Morgan, Robert J., 2011. *Then Sings My Soul, Keepsake Edition, 300 of the World's Greatest Hymn Stories, p. 357, "Beulah Land",* **W Publishing Group, An Imprint of Thomas Nelson, Nashville, Tennessee.**
*Author's note- this gives the history of the hymn mentioned in conversation only by my characters.

Hazard, W.B., M.D., Editor, *St. Louis Clinical Record, Vol. III, April 1876-7, A Monthly Journal of Medicine and Surgery,* **August 1876,** *No. 5 and* **November, 1876,** *No.8,* **p. 191, St. Louis: 1877. Accessed via eBook.**

http://www.coloradoscenicrails.com, **Georgetown Loop Railroad, "History of the Georgetown Loop Railroad"; site visited 1/23/15.** *Author's Note-This gives a wonderful timeline for the town of Georgetown from 1859 to today.

Krout, John A., Associate Professor of History Colombia University, 1941, *College Outline Series: Outline-History of the United States Since 1865 Revised, Sixth Edition,* **Barnes and Noble, Inc., New York.**

McTighe, James 1984, *Roadside History of Colorado,* **Johnson Publishing Co., Boulder, Colorado.**

Newby, Rick *2004. The Rocky Mountain Region: The Greenwood Encyclopedia of American Regional Cultures,* **Edited by Rick Newby, Forward by William Ferris, Consulting Editor, Paul S. Piper, Librarian Advisor, Greenwood Press, Westport, Connecticut. London, copyright by Rick Newby 2004**

Richards, Linda, *Reminiscences of Linda Richards: America's First Trained Nurse,* **Whitcomb and Barrows, Boston 1911, copyright 1911 by Linda Richards, Thomas Todd Co, printers, 14 Beacon Street, Boston,**

Massachusetts for Book. "The Story of This Reprint" by J.B. Lippincott Co., (Philadelphia, London, Montreal) 1948 reprint with Foreword by Anne L. Austin, Los Angeles, California as a Facsimile Reproduction; Facsimile Reprint was reproduced by Levering Riebel Co., Camden, New Jersey. Accessed via eBook/digital archive. *Author's Note- This contains information on early nursing, the first trained nurse, as well as about the female doctor, Dr. Susan Dimock, who is mentioned by name within a fictional conversation.

Roberts, Clarence N., Instructor of History, Forward written by Clarence N. Roberts, 1946. *History of the University of Missouri School of Mines and Metallurgy 1871-1946.*

Shugart, Sharon, Museum Specialist, Hot Springs National Park, *The Hot Springs of Arkansas Through the Years: A Chronology of Events- Excerpts*, Department of the Interior National Park Service, 2004. Accessed via electronic Pdf format.

Smiley, Jerome C., editor, 1901 (first edition), *History of Denver, With Outlines of the Earlier History of the Rocky Mountain Country,* The Denver Times, The Times-Sun Publishing Company, Denver 1901, Press of the Blakely Printing Co., Chicago, accessed via eBook/ digital archive

Smiley, Jerome C., edited for the Denver Times (first edition 1901- auspices of Denver

Times, second edition 1903-J.H. Williamson and Company of Denver); Index by Robert Perkin, 1971. *History of Denver, With Outlines of the Earlier History of the Rocky Mountain Country, With Many Illustrations,* special reprint edition, #72, Old Americana Publishing Company Denver, A Reproduction by UNIGRAPHIC, INC., Evansville, Indiana, 1978. *Author's Note- I borrowed this book via interlibrary loan from the University of Portland Library via the Longview Public Library. I wish to thank Taylor at the Longview Public Library for her assistance.

Swanson, Evadene B., 1975, 1993 *Fort Collins Yesterdays*, Published by Evadene Swanson.

Talbott, E.H., President and Manager, E. H. Talbott and H.R. Hobart, editors, *The Railway Age,* The Railway Age Publishing Company, Vol III., No. 6, Chicago, Thursday, February 7, 1878, Whole No. 87, p. 75, article in section "Notes From the South" from Little Rock, Ark, January 27, 1878. Accessed via EBook/digital archive. *Author's Note- the entire Volume III has wonderful research for railroad history, I have designated one portion yielding more background information on the connection to Arkansas. Volume III also has information on Colorado Railroads.

The Denver Daily Times (Denver, Colorado) Monday, 12, November 1877. Colorado Historic Newspapers Collection.

Colorado State Library
https://www.coloradohistoricnewspapers.org
(Note- author checked with the Digital Collections Coordinator, Leigh Jeremias, at the Colorado State Library on 11/30/2015 to assure correct citation listing and she approved this citation form). *Author's Note-This newspaper has an advertisement for the Kellogg-Cary Concert mentioned, as well as articles and ads reflecting the true city of Denver during this historic period. Please note my book is fiction and so are the characters attending the concert.

***The Boulder County News, Boulder, Colorado, Friday, November 9, 1877, Vol. 8, No.52,* Colorado Historic Newspapers Collection. Colorado State Library**
https://www.coloradohistoricnewspapers.org. **Site visited 4/25/16.** *Author's Note-This historic newspaper issue also advertises the upcoming Kellogg-Cary Concert and also an article about the Union Pacific Railway, advertisements for the Kansas Pacific Railway and the Colorado Central Railroad, as well as an interesting article about the extended railroad connections at that time titled, "The Colorado Central, First Through Passenger Train, Excursion to Cheyenne." This article gives a nice description and travel timeline for this period and is worth reading.

***The Colorado Transcript, Golden, Colorado, Wednesday, November 21, 1877, Volume XL,* Colorado Historic Newspapers Collection. Colorado State Library**

https://www.coloradohistoricnewspapers.org.
Site visited 4/25/16. *Author's Note-This
archive newspaper has advertisements for all the
railroad lines in the area and for my fictional
story, the connections of the Colorado Central
Railroad were of particular interest.

***The Goodspeed Biographical and
Historical Memoirs of Central Arkansas-
Pulaski, Jefferson, Lonoke, Faulkner, Grant,
Saline, Perry, Garland and Hot Springs
Counties, Arkansas.* The Goodspeed
Publishing Co., Chicago, Nashville, and St.
Louis, 1889; New Material Copyright 1978,
Southern Historical Press, The Rev. S.
Emmett Lucas, Jr., P.O., Box 738, Easley,
South Carolina 2964, Designated source
listed in book: reprinted from Original
Edition- private library of Mrs. Larry P.
Clark, Little Rock, Arkansas.** *Author's Note-
This resource yields detailed information about
the history and people of Arkansas, including
more information about the historical people
mentioned by name in the story, (*Author's
note- the mention of these places and people by
my fictional characters is only to give historical
context, scenes are fictional): Hot Springs;
Malvern; and Rockport, Arkansas; Dr. James M.
Keller, Joe "Diamond" Reynolds; and Samuel
Emerson.

An additional source for historical
information on Malvern and Rockport, Arkansas
is available via **the Hot Spring County
Historical Society,**

http://www.historicalsociety.tripod.com, and their annual publication *The Heritage.* When I first started researching this area for my first book, Brenda Matthews, a wonderful lady at the Malvern Chamber of Commerce helped in the early research process. She found multiple volumes of this publication helpful for locating the history of this wonderful area, especially **Volumes II, 4, V, VII, VIII, XV, and XXIV.** I have family from this area, so it holds a special place in my heart.

ABOUT THE AUTHOR

Lana Lynne Higginbotham (writes in the fiction genre under the pen name: *Lana* Lynne): Lana is a Speech-Language Pathologist and a writer/author. She is the author of these historical fiction novels under her pen name, Lana Lynne: *Home Always Beckons: A New Sunrise (*First Publication 2009; Revised Edition coming in 2018); Trails of Change: A New Sunset* (First Publication 2010; Revised Edition coming in 2018); and *Sunbeams at Twilight: A Life's Echo (First* Publication 2012-first printing 2012, second printing 2014, Revised Edition coming in 2018). *A Compass of Stars in Your Eyes (*First Publication 2018) is her newest historical fiction romance.

Her first contemporary Christian novella is *Whimsy Michaels and Her Amazing Room (*First publication 2018).

Other writing credits: A creative nonfiction novel, written with a coauthor: *Life Between the Letters: The Chuck and Mary Felder Story (*First Publication 2014) by Lana Lynne Higginbotham and Mary K. Felder. Blog writer: a weekly blog post (2012-2014) contributor and served as part of the "Venture Galleries Author Collection" blog team (2013) under her pen name, Lana Lynne.

Lana lives with her husband in East Texas. They are

empty nesters and proud grandparents. Learn more by visiting www.lanalynne.com.